REDEMPTION

A Father's Fatal Decision

GWEN M. PLANO

REDEMPTION

A Father's Fatal Decision

GWEN M. PLANO

Fresh Ink Group
Guntersville

Redemption

Fresh Ink Group
An Imprint of:
The Fresh Ink Group, LLC
1021 Blount Avenue #931
Guntersville, AL 35976
Email: info@FreshInkGroup.com
FreshInkGroup.com

Edition 1.0 2023

Cover by Stephen Geez / FIG
Cover art by Anik / FIG
Book design by Amit Dey / FIG
Associate publisher Beem Weeks / FIG

Cataloging-in-Publication Recommendations:
FIC042060 Fiction / Christian / Suspense
FIC042080 Fiction / Christian / Fantasy
FIC030000 Fiction / Thrillers / Suspense

Library of Congress Control Number: 2022912565

ISBN-13: 978-1-958922-16-3 Papercover
ISBN-13: 978-1-958922-17-0 Hardcover
ISBN-13: 978-1-958922-18-7 Ebooks

"True redemption is...when guilt leads to good."

— Khaled Hosseini

ACKNOWLEDGEMENTS

REDEMPTION: A Father's Fatal Decision is a piece of fiction written out of the author's imagination. New York and Connecticut are real states with real people, but the events described, characters developed, and places visited are purely fictional with no intent to depict reality.

The real folks are those who worked diligently behind the scenes to bring *REDEMPTION* to readers. From the encouragement and support of my loving husband to the remarkable assistance of my editor, and the expertise and dedication of the team at Fresh Ink Group, for all who were involved, my heartfelt *Thank You.*

TABLE OF CONTENTS

CHAPTER 1

For Lisa Holmes, this should have been a short visit. Earlier that day, her mother had called and asked her to come home, as well as reminding Lisa it had been several months since she'd last seen her daughter. Full of guilt, at that moment, she gives in against her better judgment. "I'll be home in a few hours."

The drive from upstate New York to New Rochelle is an easy one. Lisa doesn't mind the hours on the road. It's the visit itself she dreads—the inevitable interrogation from her father and the neediness of her mother. But today, she's committed to coming, and there is no turning back.

Reluctantly, Lisa throws a change of clothes into her overnight bag and puts it into her blue Toyota Camry. She plops her laptop on the seat beside her, pulls back her long dark curls, and heads south. Her thoughts comfort her, *It's just for the weekend. I can manage that. Two nights and I'll return to my apartment.*

Lisa drives with the radio blaring and ignores her apprehension. When she reaches the tree-lined street and sees the uneven sidewalk, which leads to her family's home, she smiles. Memories of her skateboard adventures ease some of her concerns. She chuckles over her many falls and imagines she must have set a record. When she arrives at their driveway, she braces herself and turns in.

The simple ranch-style residence appears odd on the street of two-story colonials. Modest by neighborhood standards, it has proven sufficient for their family needs. Once out of the car, Lisa does a 180-degree glance about and concludes nothing has changed. The yard still appears unkempt, the window shade still broken, and the screen door remains torn—all just as a year ago, two years ago, maybe even five years ago.

Apprehensive, she climbs the three steps to the front door, calls in her "hello," and waits. Mom greets her first.

"Oh, Lisa dear, I'm so happy you've arrived safely. Come on in, come on in. Can I get you something? You must be hungry after the drive."

Just as she starts to respond, her dad appears.

"Nice of you to visit. Traffic problems?"

Lisa shrugs off his insinuation of dawdling, takes a deep breath, and gives him a cursory hug.

"I'll be right back. I need to get my clothes."

Slump-shouldered, Lisa walks to her car, stepping more heavily than usual. After grabbing her suitcase, she slams the door shut. The hell has begun.

She retraces her steps back into the house and goes straight to her childhood bedroom. Just then, the doorbell rings and sends an eerie chill down Lisa's spine. She drops her suitcase and shouts to her father, "Don't answer the door, Dad. Something's not right."

He doesn't follow her advice, and instead, goes to the door and pulls it open.

"Joe." Her dad says, shifting backward slowly. "You're not supposed to be here. We agreed."

"You broke that agreement. Where is it?"

"I don't have it."

"You were warned."

One minute.

Three shots.

And Lisa's dad lies lifeless on the worn planked floor.

Her mother screams and runs to the fallen man. The guy in the doorway shoots her as well.

Before Lisa can reach her parents, the door slams shut. She checks her father but can feel no pulse. Frantic, Lisa drops to her knees at her mother's side and finds signs of life, though blood pools beneath the frail woman's shoulder. Short of breath and pulse racing, Lisa runs to the bedroom, grabs her phone, and calls 911. From the bathroom, she grabs a towel and wraps it around her mother's shoulder wound. With tears pouring down her face, Lisa holds her mom and cries out, "Please God, please God, save my mother."

An empty house is never truly vacant. Walls whisper and floors moan. It lives, even though others might not.

Lisa experiences this truth when she returns to her family home after being with her mother at the hospital. Her hand trembles as she turns the key in the front-door lock. She hesitates before entering, takes a deep, slow breath, walks inside, and turns on the light. Chills run down her spine, stiffening her limbs, numbing her heart. The ticking of the grandfather clock grows louder and louder in the silence. With her back against the entry door, she recoils when phantoms slip from one room to the other. She's alone but not really.

With measured steps, Lisa wanders through the house, tackling one memory after another. She locks the doors to the master bedroom and the basement, to silence the imaginary threats, and goes to her bedroom.

Paused in the doorway of her former childhood retreat, she looks around the room as though for the first time. Sparsely decorated with a couple of high school keepsakes and a framed photograph of her brother and her at a beach, it feels abandoned by life. Priscilla, her Cabbage Patch doll, sits tucked into the corner of the room. Lisa picks it up and holds the comforting toy against her chest in a tight grip. Her knees buckle, and she collapses on the bed and weeps.

CHAPTER 2

The following morning, Lisa awakens to the sound of a garbage truck thundering down the street. Confused as to where she is, she sits up. After rubbing her eyes, she glances about the space. *My bedroom. No … no … no. It can't be true. My nightmare wasn't a dream.*

Fully dressed, and still holding the doll she'd grabbed the night before, Lisa checks the time. Half past seven. In less than two hours, she must meet with an appointed psychologist. When she recalls the murder, her lips tighten. *I wasn't myself. They should have understood. I don't need counseling sessions.*

Lisa cringes when she considers her behavior. *After the police responded to her emergency call, she lashed out at the officers for not arriving sooner, for not catching the murderer, for not getting immediate help for her mother, and for not making everything better.*

As she recalls the horrifying events and her first ride in a patrol car, Lisa's head falls. *Unable to calm her, they put her in the back seat of the cruiser and took her to the station. Once there, the captain talked with her. An intimidating no-nonsense man with dark skin and piercing brown eyes, he listened to her rants, reviewed the police report, and determined that she needed professional help. He sent her home with the signed agreement that she'd attend weekly counseling sessions for two months.*

Lisa shakes her head and stares at the worn carpet at her feet. *I wasn't myself. I was in shock. They should have understood. Shouldn't they?* After a deep breath, she checks the time again and moves to ready herself for the meeting with the psychologist.

At ten minutes after nine, Lisa arrives for her first session. Begrudgingly, she knocks on the office door. A simple sign reads *Dr. Thomas Schultz, Ph.D.*

"You must be Lisa. A little late, but at least you're here. Come on in."

She glares at the bespectacled old guy with a notebook in his hand. *This will be worse than a prison cell.* She says nothing.

"I can see I've met your expectations." A sly smile betrays the psychologist's amusement. "Please, take a seat on the couch."

A chair, a couch, tissues. Perfect. What have I gotten myself into? She smirks.

"So, Lisa, I have the police report, but it's one-sided. A hysterical woman accosting innocent police officers. Sound familiar?"

Lisa responds with defiance, "Maybe."

"Let's hear your side."

Lisa straightens and considers what she wants to say. Her eyes scan the room and return to Dr. Schultz. He cocks his head to the side and waits.

"I heard the doorbell ring and, somehow, I felt danger. I'd just arrived home and was in my bedroom with the door open partially. I called out to my dad to not answer, but he did anyway. A man—tall, white, medium build—pushed his way in and shouted at my father. 'Where is it?' Dad said, 'I told you I don't have it.' Then the guy said, 'Your choice,' and shot him three times. Mom ran to his aid, and he shot her as well then left. Dad died instantly. There was no chance for goodbyes. My mom was bleeding from her shoulder. I called the police and asked for an ambulance. It seemed like hours before they arrived. I held her and tried to stop the bleeding. She couldn't move. I felt terrified. Then the police came. I yelled at them and hit them with my fists. That's when they restrained me. And at the same time, the EMTs arrived and took my mom. So there. That's my side of the story."

Dr. Schultz inhales slowly and studies Lisa before responding. "I would have done the same thing."

Lisa redirects her attention and fights her tears so as not to appear vulnerable. "It was horrifying."

"I can't imagine a scene much worse than the one you've described."

"You've experienced something similar?"

"That's a story for another day." He pauses before continuing, "I know you don't want to be here, but I promise you, if you work with me, your horror and grief will soften, and you'll find personal peace."

Lisa meets his gaze. Instinctively, she doesn't trust him. *A bold promise about which he knows nothing, and yet, he claims expertise.*

"We'll see."

"Together, we can do it. I promise."

Another promise. Lisa grows alarmed. She shrugs her agreement, checks her watch, and sinks into the sofa. There, she reaches for a tissue and stares—stony-faced—at the oak floor.

"Thank you. Let's begin with what you've told me about your side of the events. Can we do that?"

"I don't have a choice, do I?"

"I offered you the choice, and I gave you a promise. Shall we begin?"

Lisa squirms, annoyed. "I guess so."

"You've acknowledged that when the doorbell rang, you felt there was danger. Why?"

"Sometimes, I sense things. I can't explain it. Since I was a kid, I knew things—about people, about places. Sometimes I had dreams."

"Did you have a dream about this murder?"

"Yes and no. I dreamed of someone murdering Dad. I had the same dream several times, and that's why I agreed to drive down for a visit. The nightmare didn't tell me where or when, but I decided to tell my parents of my concerns. I never got to do that. The doorbell rang. I was too late."

"Did you recognize the man?"

"No. A hoody covered his hair and face. I was in another room and could only make out his nose and hands. Nothing that would help identify him."

"Your mom?"

"She can't speak. Can't move. I don't know what she saw or if she can remember that day." Lisa shifts in her seat, uncomfortable, and avoids eye contact.

"I'm deeply sorry, Lisa. This isn't something you can forget, forgive, or even ignore easily. It will live in you until the mystery gets solved and there's justice. Because of what you've seen and experienced, we might be able to help with that process. Are you ready to begin the work?"

Lisa purses her lips and stares at the psychologist. She doesn't want to proceed, but given the circumstances, she agrees.

Dr. Schultz picks up his pen and moves forward in his seat. "When you think about your dreams, do you drift into that space?"

"Sort of. I just focus on it as though it were real and don't pay attention to anything else."

"Okay. I want you to do that. I want you to drift into your dream world. When you're ready, tell me what you see."

Lisa glances out the window for a moment and shifts into a meditative state.

Schultz pushes back into his chair and watches for a change in Lisa's expression. Her lips have tightened. "Are you looking at someone?"

"Yes. A man with a gun."

"What's he doing?"

"He's pointing the gun at my dad."

"What else? Does he say anything?"

"He's angry with my dad. He wants something. Dad tells him he doesn't have it. The man says he needs to pay up. Dad gives an excuse, but the man opens fire."

"What does the attacker look like?"

Lisa stays silent, assessing the dream and the therapist. Finally, she says, "I can't see him clearly, but he has dark hair and dark eyes. White skin. He looks dirty as if he's a hands-on worker."

"What's he wearing?"

"A hoodie, black. There's a design on it, or perhaps, smeared grease. His jeans are old and snug on his legs."

"What about the weapon?"

"I don't know guns, but this one is black with a short barrel."

"How does your father appear?"

Lisa's tone changes when she looks at her dad. "He seems small compared to this man. And weak. He talks fast as though he's worried. He knows this person—calls him Joe."

Lisa shudders and straightens against the couch.

"What's wrong?"

"That's what Dad called the killer. Joe."

"With your dream in mind, go to the murder scene. Stand behind your father. What do you see?"

"The same man in my dream." Lisa falls silent and takes another tissue from the box.

"Does he see you?"

"Doubt it. He was in and out. I was in my old bedroom, and the door to the room was only slightly ajar. He never looked in my direction. After he fired, he fled. It was over in less than a minute, maybe two."

"What could you have done to protect your parents?"

Lisa's fists tighten and her lips contort. "There was NOTHING I could have done! That's why I reacted so badly to the police." Her eyes widen and she looks down at the floor. She glances at Schultz and meets his eyes.

Schultz nods his agreement. "Exactly. There was nothing you could have done to help them."

Lisa's hands quiver when she wipes away her copious tears. "I would have. Truly, I would have if I could have."

Dr. Schultz lays his pen on his notebook and puts a hand to his chin but says nothing. After a few seconds, he speaks, "We've accomplished a lot today. This is a good place to stop. Are you okay with that?"

"Yes."

"Do you have any questions for me?"

"These sessions are confidential, right?"

"Absolutely. No one is privy to what transpires in my office. No one. My personal and professional contract is with you alone." He pauses and considers an idea. "I have an assignment for you. On the shelf across from your armrest, there's a book with a brown cover."

"I see it."

"Take it home with you. It has images of eyes, noses, mouths, and ears. I want you to page through the photos and select those that remind you of the shooter in your dreams."

Lisa opens the book and flips through the pages. She sits back. "Okay, I'll do it."

"When we meet next week, we'll review the composite. For now, I want you to keep a notebook with you. Here's one you can use." He hands her a blank notebook. "Jot down any image, situation, or memory that comes up. And if you have another dream, write it out in detail. Are you okay with that?"

She looks down at the notebook and back up. "Yes, sir."

He stands, strides to the door, and opens it. Lisa follows.

"I'll see you in a week."

Schultz closes the door behind her.

CHAPTER 3

Time passes quickly for those longing for more, but for others, it can disappear into the night, where it lingers and haunts. Lisa experiences the latter.

She sits on the steps that lead to the backyard and sips her morning brew, her eyes red and raw from another sleepless night. It's been over a week since a man murdered her father, and today is his funeral. A glance at her watch shows Lisa it's time for her to leave.

Alone, Lisa drives to the burial ground. Her brother cannot attend because he's out of the country. Her mother will arrive via hospital transport. *Will anyone else be there?*

After Lisa turns onto the cemetery drive, she grips the steering wheel and bites her lower lip. She reduces her speed to a crawl and edges over to her father's plot. When she spots the priest, she parks and walks to his side.

"You don't need to worry about anything, Ms. Holmes," he says. "I'll guide you through the ceremony."

"Thank you, Father. This is the first funeral I've attended, and I'm not familiar with the process."

"I understand. Just focus on your mom. Katherine needs you now. Don't worry about the rest." He turns his head to the side. "I see she's arrived."

A medical transport van parks near the site. Lisa excuses herself and goes to help her mother.

Expressionless, Lisa stares at her father's casket—dark mahogany wood with gold trim. For years, she's thought about this moment and wondered how he might die. The tears well, but she's not sure why. *Did I love him, after all?*

Sniffles sound from among those seated on the grassy knoll, which prompts Lisa to question what's in her heart. *Maybe it's regret. Maybe it's for a childhood that never was. Maybe it's just because. Doesn't everyone cry at funerals?*

She takes her mom's hand, cold and lifeless as it is, and holds it in a firm clasp. A single bullet to the thoracic area of her spine has stolen her agile life. Her mother neither speaks nor moves, yet counter to her functional deficits, a tear runs down her cheek. Lisa wipes it away and adjusts her mom's collar. After she wraps her arm around her mother's shoulders, Lisa focuses on the priest, who stands to the side of the casket and mouths a prayer. She hears nothing except the pounding of her heart. *Who shot my father? Does anyone have any answers?* Memories of earlier years flash before her—images of the father she both feared and, perhaps, loved.

A pallbearer jars her into the present with two words, "It's time."

Lisa remembers the instructions and rises. Like a windup doll, she lifts the arrangement of red chrysanthemums and white daisies, lays it on the casket, and draws a breath. *Why can't I feel anything?* With a sigh, Lisa moves next to the priest. Beside him, she looks over at her mother, listless in a wheelchair with an oxygen tube at her throat. *Dad didn't pull the trigger, but he did this to her, to us. I should at least be able to feel hate.*

A few minutes later, the cleric touches her hand and nods. It's time for her to say a prayer. Dutifully, Lisa eases herself to the casket side and bends to kiss its cold surface. She mouths a silent prayer and turns to gaze at those gathered to offer their respects.

"Thank you for your kindness. My mother and I are grateful for your presence with us today."

Someone sobs, and Lisa swivels to see an Asian woman about her own age wiping away tears. *Who is she? The latest lover?* Lisa exhales slowly and returns to her seat.

The priest says a final prayer for Eric W. Holmes and sprinkles holy water on his casket. Lisa's attention drifts to the raven perched on the limb of an oak tree several yards away. His caw helps her stay focused on the funeral. She checks her watch. *It's been thirty-five minutes but seems like hours.*

At the end of the service, several people saunter past Lisa and Katherine and pause to express condolences. *Are they sincere or just going through the motions? Does anyone care that my dad's dead?* When she remembers the murder, her lips tighten. *I want to go home and forget it ever happened.*

Lisa stands and motions to the caregiver, a young man in a white jacket, and says, "Time to leave." She reaches to help the attendant but, instead, helplessness overwhelms her. The aide moves methodically and slowly while he pushes the wheelchair to the van. When the electronic lift raises Katherine into the vehicle, Lisa again hears the haunting caw of a raven.

"I'll see you in a few minutes, Mom." Lisa kisses Katherine's forehead and waits for a response. None comes. She steps back and watches the van pull away. Her shoulders fall, and she wipes away fresh tears. *I've lost my mother as well.*

Once in the car, Lisa heads to Interstate 95 and makes a quick side trip to their family home before going to the hospital. When she approaches the front door, she observes multiple cards positioned behind the screen. Lisa sighs. *I can't deal with this right now.* She removes the cards and enters the house.

Lisa stands in the doorway and detects the dry residue of blood, still visible on the planked floor. She tosses the sympathy cards on the side table and drags a runner rug from the living room to cover the lingering evidence. A wave of nausea washes over her, and she runs to the bathroom. At the sink, Lisa splashes water on her swollen face. Her panting breaths make her feel faint. *I must stay calm. I can do this. I can.* A glance into the mirror shows her mother staring back at her. Will her mom walk or talk again? Lisa grimaces. *If Mom needs me, I'll arrange a leave of absence from work and move to New Rochelle.* With a deep breath, Lisa cups her face in her hands and weeps.

Ten minutes later, red-faced but determined, Lisa exits the house and takes the freeway to the hospital. She pounds on the steering wheel with the palms of her hands as she drives and shouts, "Why, Dad? Why? How could you let this happen?"

At the hospital, Lisa comes to a screeching halt, and her anguish builds as the questions mount. She relives the shooting again and again. Still no answers. After climbing out of the car, she shoves the door shut.

Lisa sucks in one deep inhalation and another and turns to face the hospital entrance. She dreads walking through those glass revolving doors and ignores the shiver running through her veins. After signing in at the front desk, she steps into the elevator and travels to the second floor—room 211. At the doorway of her mother's room, she peeks inside and braces for the encounter.

Katherine lies motionless on the adjustable bed and stares at the ceiling with a blank expression. Upon seeing this, Lisa's head falls. *It's been nine days since the shooting, and still, nothing has changed. Does she even remember the funeral this morning?* Lisa flinches and walks in.

"Hi, Mom. I'm here." Lisa pushes a chair close to the bed and takes her mother's hand. *So pale*, she thinks. *Even the veins can't hide*. Gently, she leans to kiss her on the cheek, but her once vibrant mother doesn't even blink—her big blue eyes devoid of life.

"I thought it was a beautiful funeral this morning, didn't you? The flowers were perfect, just as you would have wanted." Lisa pauses, and silence echoes throughout the room. "I recognized a couple of the neighbors. It was kind of them to come. Most people I didn't know, perhaps you did?" Lisa looks down at the linoleum floor as sadness builds.

She strokes her mother's slender fingers. "I love you, Mom. I wish I knew that you could hear me." When she sees no sign of awareness, Lisa continues her one-sided chat, "I fed the hummingbirds this morning. It was the first time I really watched them. It's amazing how they can fly in all directions, even backward. No wonder you love them so much." Lisa searches for any sign of consciousness but finds none. "I also watered the daisies. I've put a vase of them beside your bed. Did you see them?"

After a short pause, Lisa inhales and changes the subject. "I got an award for the findings on the Smyth audit. My boss said he'd never seen such clever work." She stops speaking, and her chin trembles. Tears rim her eyes and will soon cascade down her cheeks. Katherine hasn't moved at all.

Lisa tries one more time and mentions her older brother, "Mom, Trace called today. He's so sorry he couldn't be here for you." At those words, Lisa observes movement around her mother's eyes. She shifts in her chair to better watch the reactions and continues, "Trace said he's flying back from Tel Aviv in three days, and after he drops off his bags, he'll come to the hospital." Again, Lisa sees a reflex from her mom. "He loves you dearly." At that comment, Lisa watches a tear form at the side of her mother's eye. She scoots her chair backward. "I'll be right back." Lisa dashes to the hallway to find a nurse.

"Please come," Lisa says. "My mom can understand. She's reacting to what I say."

The nurse follows Lisa inside and speaks in a focused manner to Katherine. The uniformed woman watches intently but sees no reaction and tightens her lips. "I'm sorry, but there's no indication she's alert."

"Wait! Watch her eyes when I speak to her."

Lisa turns to her mom and says, "Trace is flying in to be with you, Mom. I'll pick him up at the airport the day after tomorrow."

This time the nurse notices fluttering around the eyelids. "I'll get the doctor."

Within minutes, Dr. Rodriguez arrives. Lisa pulls her aside to explain what she's witnessed and share some of the family dynamics.

"My mom is protective of Trace because my father treated him poorly. He hasn't visited home for years. For the last two weeks, he's been out of the country and missed the funeral. When Mom heard Trace's name, she moved her eyes."

Dr. Rodriguez nods her understanding. "Thank you for sharing a little of your family history. This may help with her treatment." The physician turns and walks over to her patient.

"Mrs. Holmes, may I call you Katherine? My name is Dr. Rodriguez. I've heard you're showing signs of awareness. This is great news. It seems you and I have a lot in common. We both have a son. Because I'm a single mother, I depend on my son for everything. Your daughter mentioned your son will be here soon. Trace, right?"

The doctor and Lisa both see a reaction. "You love him dearly, don't you?"

Katherine's eyes widen and flicker.

Dr. Rodriguez says, "You're like me, Katherine. I tried to protect my son. You did too, didn't you?"

Tears pool in Katherine's eyes.

The doctor says, "You saved him from his father." After a glance at Lisa, she looks back at her patient. "You're a brave woman, Katherine, and you're stronger than you imagine. Soon, you'll be with your children again in your own home. It will take some work, but I know you can do it, and I will help you every step of the way."

The doctor motions for Lisa to join her outside the room.

"Your mom hears, and she can respond to emotional stimuli. I'll order a full neuro workup. One of my associates is a leading neurosurgeon at NY Presbyterian in Tarrytown. I'll give him a call. There's hope—how much, I don't know, but there's hope."

CHAPTER 4

In the driver's seat, Lisa slouches and tips her head back, momentarily closing her eyes. She wrings her hands and thinks about her mom's condition and the thread of hope the doctor offered. After turning the ignition key, she circles out to the freeway and switches on the radio. Loud. Along with the pounding music, Lisa screams her frustration and almost misses her exit. Panicked, she overcorrects and slips to the side of the ramp.

At a standstill, Lisa pants and darts nervous glances out the windows. Once she's eased back onto the ramp, she pauses longer than usual at the stop sign. She begins again, more slowly this time, down the familiar road, and to her driveway. Lisa pulls in and comes to an abrupt stop. The front door hangs open.

Afraid to get out of the car, she calls 911. "Someone has broken into my house. Yes. I'll wait."

The response to her call comes immediately, and within a couple of minutes, a police cruiser pulls in behind her, and two officers get out.

"I arrived just a few minutes ago and saw this." She points to the front door of her mother's home.

"Did you go into the house or see anyone leave it?"

"No, sir. I was afraid to get out of my car. Less than two weeks ago, someone killed my father when he opened that door."

"Stay put. We'll check it out."

Each of the officers takes out a Glock sidearm and approaches the door cautiously. Another patrol car arrives. The lead officer signals for the other uniforms to circle to the back of the building.

While keeping her focus on the front door, Lisa hugs her ribs and rocks back and forth.

After several minutes, an officer walks over to Lisa and tells her, "It's safe to enter. Be prepared, though, as the intruders ransacked the house. He, or they, seems to have been looking for something specific. Do you have security cameras?"

"I'm not sure. I haven't lived here for five years."

"Not a problem. If your parents had them installed, we'll find them."

Lisa exits her car, turns and takes a step toward the front door. A neighbor approaches the police, and Lisa pauses to listen.

"Officer?" The stranger calls out.

"Yes?"

"I live across the street. Dan Sampson. Can I help?"

"Did you see anything?"

"Yes, a dark-blue SUV pulled in about an hour ago. On the side of the van, it read *Jameson Movers*. Three guys got out. I tried to get the license, but I only saw the last three numbers—eight-three-seven."

"Which state?"

"New York." Sampson looks at the ground. "I should have called you guys, but I thought the family was moving."

"Do you have security cameras?"

"I do."

"We'll need the videos from them."

"I'll cooperate in any way I can. This is a quiet community, officer. We've never had anything like this happen before. Everyone in the cul-de-sac is shocked by the murder and now this."

"What do you know about the victim, Eric Holmes?"

"Not much. Eric seemed like a good guy but was rarely here. Other than *hello*, I don't believe I've ever spoken with him. I do know his wife, Katherine. When we'd have neighborhood gatherings, she always participated. She's a kind woman. I sure hope she's recovering well."

"So you know your neighbors?"

"All of them."

The officer motions to a subordinate to come over. "Officer Wong, check the surveillance videos at each of the surrounding houses. Dan is a neighbor. You can start with his. We need as much information about these intruders as we can get."

"I'm on it, sir."

Lisa follows a female officer down the pathway. When she steps into the house, Lisa freezes. Furniture lies in complete disorder, with stuffing pulled from upholstery, paintings tossed on the floor, and walls ripped open. In a stupor, she swallows hard and trudges through the room. A broken end table causes her to stumble, and she balances against the wall before reaching the bedroom that had been her childhood sanctuary.

Lisa covers her mouth and, feeling unsteady, grabs hold of the door casing. The desecration is complete. Her bed, stripped naked, heaves chunks of foam through multiple gashes. Her closet, bare of clothes, exposes ruptured walls. Her stored childhood memories, scattered across the floor, scream for her attention.

In a daze, Lisa sits on the edge of her bed and picks up a t-shirt and a comb. She holds them close to her. A broken picture frame with one of her high school achievements stares up at her from her feet. When she looks at it, terror creeps through her body, and her heartbeat thrashes in her ears. "This can't be happening," she mutters.

A man's voice shouts from the basement, calling for the captain. A large, burly officer hurries past her doorway and stomps down the wooden steps to the partially finished space. Lisa follows. As she descends, she sees another officer pointing to a hole in the sheetrock. "Captain, it looks like the intruders pulled a safe from the wall. It fit snugly between the studs."

The captain turns and looks surprised to see Lisa. "We met at the station last week, ma'am. Remember?"

"Yes, sir."

"By chance, do you know what was in the safe?"

"No. I only remember my mom saying it protected important documents because it was fireproof."

Petrified, she stands in place, rigid. The captain stares at her, and she at him—both midway down the stairs. "I realize I didn't even know my parents."

The captain studies her and suggests she go upstairs. "Ma'am, I'll join you in a minute and explain what we're going to do."

Lisa takes his advice and wanders upward and through to the kitchen, the dining room, and—finally—to the living room. She finds nothing to sit on so returns to her bedroom, clutches a pillow lying on the floor, and holds it tight. Exhausted and overwrought, she collapses on the side of the broken bed.

The captain walks into the rubble and finds Lisa sobbing in a fetal position next to mounds of foam bedding. He clears his throat. "Ma'am?"

Lisa sits up and looks at the towering officer.

"Ma'am, I'll do everything I can to find the criminals who did this to you and your family. I'm assigning an investigative team to this case. This isn't a typical break-in. The thieves are looking for something specific, and unless they found what they wanted, they'll be back. Do you know when this occurred?"

"I, ahh, I was at the hospital this afternoon, and when I got home, I found this." She points across the room.

"So, during the hour or two that you were gone, someone broke in? Interesting. They might be watching the house—and you."

Lisa's mouth falls open.

"You can't stay here. Until we close this case, you need around-the-clock protection. I've secured permission to assign a detail to your case. He or she carries a photo ID, so you can ask to see it, just to be sure."

Lisa tries to process what he says. She squints and furrows her brow. "Protection?" She glances around. "My brother flies in this evening. I think he can protect me. Maybe I should ask him."

"You don't know who or what you're up against, ma'am. I can't stress strongly enough that both you and your brother are targets. You're not safe. Get what you need out of the house now and stay clear of it. Do you have a place you can go?"

"No. Neither my brother nor I live in this area anymore. We need to stay close to our mom. That's all I know for sure."

"If you're staying local, I can help. Do you remember my name?" At her obvious confusion, he continues, "Captain Davis. Consider me your contact as we go forward. Here's my card." He holds out a small rectangular card, and Lisa takes it. "Call me if anything comes up. Can you do that?"

"Yes, sir."

"First matter of business, we must find a place for you to stay. The Westchester Tower has worked with me on other cases. I'll call them, and you and your brother can go there. I'll get back to you with the details. What's your phone number?"

Mechanically, Lisa recites her number and her brother's and watches Captain Davis enter them into his cell. A slow inhale helps her feel a sense of security in knowing that the captain will help. She lifts her eyes and meets his. "Thank you, sir. I'll try to find some clothes in this mess and get out of your way."

Lisa sets her suitcase on the bed and looks in all directions—from corner to corner and pile to pile. Tears trail down her cheeks, and fear and disbelief tighten her throat. She spots a crumpled t-shirt, then a pair of jeans, and throws both into her suitcase. After spying her bag of toiletries and vitamins on the floor, she packs those as well. Then she pauses. The voices in the other rooms fade, and suddenly, she's a little girl again. She remembers … a dream. She's seen this wreckage before. In a panic, Lisa looks for her Cabbage Patch doll. *It must be here. It has to be here.* Frantic, she searches under the pile of blankets and books and school reports, and … there it is. Priscilla. Intact. Flooded with relief, Lisa tucks the doll into the suitcase, perplexed as to why it feels critical to do so, and marches out of the house.

Neighbors gather in the front yard and tell the police what they saw and heard. Lisa doesn't want to talk to them. Not now. Maybe never. After giving them a quick wave, she focuses on the worn path to her car. Once inside the illusory safety of the vehicle, she exhales slowly and backs out of the driveway, around the patrol cars, through the well-wishers, and onto the street. The sight of the neighbors talking with the police and sharing their security camera information helps her feel safe. *They'll find the perpetrators. I'll be okay.*

The drive to the Westchester Tower Hotel takes twenty minutes. The building sits near the county airport, where her brother will soon land, and it's a short drive from there to the hospital. While she speeds down the freeway, barely aware of the busy commuter traffic and the truck that honks and wants to pass, Lisa obsesses about the vandalized house, her mother's condition, and her doll. The latter holds Lisa's attention most strongly. *Why is Priscilla so important?*

As she maneuvers into a parking space at the hotel, Lisa checks her watch—half past five. *I have time to freshen up.* After yanking the keys from the ignition, she drops them as she steps out of the car. When Lisa reaches for the key ring, she finds a little black box attached to the underside of the wheel well. She struggles to dislodge it from the car frame, but—finally—the device snaps loose. Lisa examines it and adds the contraption to the list of things she wants to discuss with Trace. Once she's shoved it into her purse, Lisa snatches the suitcase and her laptop from the car and walks to the front desk.

"Your name, please?"

"Lisa Holmes."

"Welcome, Ms. Holmes. Captain Davis reserved a suite for you on the sixth floor. Here are your room keys and your designated parking spaces." The receptionist hands her two plastic key cards and reels off the room number. "Two bedrooms, two baths. It overlooks the city and the mountains to the north. You'll appreciate the view, especially from the deck. Please call if you have any special requests."

Lisa thanks the clerk and steps into the elevator, preoccupied with everything happening in her life. A man of about her age enters behind her. They stand silently as the elevator moves, then Lisa spots a badge sticking out from the man's jacket pocket, and takes a leap, "Are you the police officer assigned to my case?"

He clears his throat and shifts awkwardly. "Affirmative."

"I'd like to look at your photo identification."

The guy reaches into his side pocket for his credentials and gives it to Lisa.

"Officer Leonard, it appears we'll be seeing a lot of each other."

"Hopefully, I won't be visible."

"Hmm, I suspect it's unavoidable that we notice one another."

"Ma'am, I'll do my best to protect you from any threat."

"That's good to know. It's a scary situation, and one I've never faced before."

The elevator jerks to a halt, and they both step out. She wants to hug him but doesn't know why. Instead, she opts for the accepted conduct and extends her hand. "Nice to meet you, officer. Thank you for your help."

"I'm here for you, ma'am—just across the hall."

"That's reassuring, sir. If someone tries to break into my suite, I know you'll give chase." She smiles. "Have a good evening."

Once in the unit, Lisa latches the door and rests against it to survey the room. The bay of floor-to-ceiling windows opposite the entrance captures her attention. She sets her laptop on the coffee table and leaves her suitcase by the door. After walking to the windows, she opens the sliding door and inhales the brisk air. Stepping outside, Lisa looks across the horizon and down to the garden far below. She takes a seat in one of the cushioned patio chairs and lets her face fall into her palms. The hoot of an owl quiets her tears. When she looks up, Lisa tries to find it among the treetops. With a deep, cleansing breath, she tells herself, *This is my home now.*

After a few minutes, she goes back into the suite and explores the rooms. She's never stayed in a hotel with accommodations of this caliber. Lisa claims one of the bedrooms and rolls in her suitcase. She dumps its contents onto the vast, sumptuous bed and spots her doll. *What is it about you, Priscilla? What's the secret you hold?*

Lisa puts away her clothes and opts for a quick nap. As she drifts into a restless sleep, a dream jars her to wakefulness. She sees herself in a car with her father, and trees zoom past. Her feet don't touch the floor, and she kicks them playfully as they travel. She holds Priscilla and whispers to her, but her dad tells her to be quiet. Something is wrong. He looks scary. They're going somewhere far away, somewhere secluded, but she doesn't remember where. Lisa sits up and rubs her eyes. *I must focus on this memory. It might explain why Priscilla is important.*

Lisa checks the time and jumps and grabs her keys. *I've got to pick up Trace at the airport. He's due in fifteen minutes.*

At the door, she startles when her cell phone rings.

Captain Davis greets her, "Are you settled in, ma'am?"

"Yes, sir. Thank you. It's a lovely suite."

"Great. We've got you covered. I've assigned an officer to your case, and he has a room across the hall from you. I'll make sure someone stays nearby until this situation is resolved. As a reminder, if you contact an officer, ask the person to show you their photo ID. In general, they should be invisible."

"I appreciate that, sir. I've met Officer Leonard already."

"Good. You can depend on him."

"Anything else to tell me?"

"I'm not sure what you mean, but in terms of the house, we found nothing. There must be another hiding spot. We've alerts out on the SUV and its occupants. Hopefully, we'll have good news soon, and when we do, you'll be the first to know."

"Thank you, sir. I appreciate it."

CHAPTER 5

Lisa circles the Westchester County Airport and parks in the cell phone waiting area. She checks the electronic message board for incoming flights and realizes she's a few minutes early. After pushing back into her seat, she peers into her rearview mirror and sees Officer Leonard. Another car pulls into the lot. The middle-aged female driver looks vaguely familiar, but Lisa cannot place her.

While tapping her fingers on the steering wheel, Lisa frets about what she'll say to Trace. *Where do I begin? The murder, the funeral, Mom's condition, or the destruction at the house? This will be a long night.*

Overhead, an engine roars, and a passenger plane descends. The message board shows an announcement for the arrival of Trace's flight. Lisa turns on the ignition and backs out of the waiting space to look for a parking spot near the arrival gate. She finds a place opposite the arrival exit, parks, and stands next to her car.

With a backpack thrown across his left shoulder, Trace spots Lisa and hurries to greet her, "Hey, sis. You're a welcome sight." He buries her in a big hug. "Are those tears, I see? Everything will be okay. Trust me."

"It's been a hellish week, but now that you're here, I know we'll get through this."

"You can count on it. I'm ready for anything. I wish I could have made the funeral—if nothing else to help you, but I couldn't get away. I was mid-project, and the supervisor ... you know how it goes."

"Yeah. I understand completely."

"But I'm here now. One hundred percent." He gives her a mischievous shove. "So, what's on the itinerary first? I know you've got everything planned for my visit."

Lisa chuckles. "You know me too well. For a starter, I thought we'd visit Mom before it gets too late."

"I'm all for that." His voice lowers. "How's she doing?"

"I'll explain once we're on our way."

They get into the car and buckle up. Trace looks at her. "So … tell me. How is she?"

"Not so great, but there are glimmers of hope now. A couple of days ago, I told her you were flying in to be with her, and her eyes fluttered. That sounds minor, but her response showed she could understand. I called for the doctor, and she talked to Mom about her son and how she loved him and tried to protect him. Mom's eyes watered, Trace. She's aware."

"Thank God." Trace tightens his hands. "This whole mess breaks my heart, and I can't help but blame Dad. This happened because of him."

"Well, we have a lot to talk about, but first, Mom. We should reach the hospital in five. She can't move, so brace yourself. It's not a pretty scene. But after the doctor witnessed her response to your name, she agreed to contact one of her friends, a leading New York neurosurgeon. Mom will have a full neurological exam."

"I regret not being here. Maybe I could have done something to prevent the murder."

"Impossible. The whole drama lasted a minute, two at most. It happened that fast."

Lisa maneuvers into a parking space and jerks to a stop.

"Hmm, some things haven't changed."

"Oh, good grief! You're dumping on me about my driving NOW?"

"Just wanted to see that smile. Okay, let's go check on Mom."

As they near the entrance, Trace takes her hand and lifts it. "Remember what she would say about my brown skin and your white? 'You two are like chocolate and vanilla. You can't have one without the other.' We're in this together, Lisa. If necessary, I'll use vacation time. I've got plenty, especially after this last assignment."

Lisa leads the way to Katherine's room on the second floor. Once there, Trace leans to peek around the door pane and backs away. With tight lips, he turns to Lisa. "Now I understand what you meant. Let's both take a deep breath and go in together."

Trace and Lisa move to their mother's side. Her adjustable bed tilts upwards at a thirty-degree angle. An IV pole stands beside the bed, and a tube runs from the hanging bag into Katherine's arm.

"Mom, it's Trace. I'm here beside you."

Her eyes flutter as though she's trying to open them.

"I'm staying for a while to help you and Lisa. Don't worry about anything. We'll handle everything." He reaches for his mother's hand and kisses it. "I've missed you, more than you know. I'll be home more frequently now."

A tear rolls down her cheek.

"It's been hard, hasn't it? You've done your best through the years, and I'm grateful for all the ways you helped and protected me. Anything I've achieved is because of you. I love you, Mom." He bends over, sets his forehead down next to hers, and lets his tears fall.

Lisa chokes back her emotion and notices her mom's fingers. She gets Trace's attention and points to the movement. They watch as the index finger on their mother's right hand moves up and down.

Trace puts Katherine's hand in his and rubs it. "Remember when I fell from the oak tree behind our house? My hand got pretty messed up. I had trouble moving my fingers because of the swelling. You sat beside me and put compresses on and kept telling me I'd be okay. And after two or three days, I was. Now it's my turn. You'll be okay. It may take a few extra days, but you'll be fine."

Katherine's fingers lift and fall, lift and fall.

Trace smiles broadly and looks over at Lisa, who holds her hand over her mouth in astonishment.

"Remember the song you would sing to Lisa and me?" Trace clears his throat and begins, "He's got the whole world in His hands, He's got the whole world in His hands, He's got the whole world in His hands ..."

Lisa moves closer. Their mom moves her lips—trying to sing.

"He's got everybody here in His hands ... Mom, you're in His hands. You'll walk out of here with Lisa on one side of you and me on the other."

A nurse stands at the door, and Trace nods that he understands it's time to leave.

"Mom, the nurse just let us know you need to rest. We'll say good night, but we'll come back in the morning. You sleep well, and maybe tomorrow we can all sing a song or two." He bends and kisses her.

Lisa follows his lead, and whispers, "I love you."

Trace and Lisa proceed out of the building with their heads lowered. Trace mutters something unintelligible and hits his fist into his other hand. "It's his fault, you do know that, right?"

"Yeah, I know it. I can't prove it, but I know it." She backs out of the parking space. "I need to show you something."

"There's more yet to see?"

"Mom's a casualty of a bigger mess. It's probably better to let you see for yourself and then explain."

"Well, now you have me worried, but okay."

They pass the remainder of the short drive in silence. When they arrive at their childhood home, two police cars sit in the driveway. Trace turns a questioning look at Lisa. "What the hell?"

"I told you there was more. Leave your suitcase in the car. We're not staying here."

Trace hurries to the front door, but an officer stops him from entering. Lisa shouts, "He's my brother. We just came from the hospital."

After Trace produces his ID for the police officer, he and Lisa step into the house. Trace recoils and gasps. "Oh, my God. What happened?"

"The short version is three thugs came in and tore the place up, looking for an unidentified object, presumably the thing for which they killed Dad."

Trace's jaw drops. "I can't believe this." Distracted, he walks from one room to the next. The veins on his neck bulge with growing frustration. Lisa follows and tries to explain what occurred and how the investigation is proceeding.

Trace blurts out, "Why didn't you call me?"

"You were boarding a plane."

"You could have left a message."

"And what would I have said that would have made any difference?"

"I don't know. How would anyone describe this catastrophe?"

As Trace looks around the room, his face reddens with anger. He opens and closes his fists. "I'd like to hit one of these walls myself." Stepping into his former bedroom, he snags some football memorabilia and baseball cards and throws them across the littered area.

"Did they get what they were looking for?"

"The police believe not, which is why we're under protective custody."

"You're kidding me."

"No. Did you notice the car that pulled in after we arrived?"

Trace looks out the window to the driveway and shakes his head in baffled confusion. "Is there anything more you haven't told me?"

"We'll talk about that later."

"Let's get out of here."

Trace storms through the front door, with Lisa fast behind him. As she runs past the officers, she says thank you and climbs into the car.

"Where are you taking me? Do you have more surprises? Another freak show, perhaps?"

"We have a temporary home at a hotel. You'll like it. You have your own room and bathroom."

"We don't have a home, Lisa. Temporary or otherwise. Dad took everything with him—except us, and I'll not let him take us with him."

Lisa enters the hotel lot, parks, and faces Trace. "He won't get us, but we may get him. I don't want to leave any stone unturned, and I'm determined to find the underlying reasons for this mess. I want to know what Dad participated in that destroyed our family. I hope you're with me on this."

"Are you serious? Whatever it takes."

Trace follows Lisa to the sixth floor. She hands him the extra card key. "We're right here." He unlocks the door and walks into the suite.

"Whoa, nice quarters."

"I said you'd like it. Your bedroom's to the left. I've claimed mine already."

Lisa throws her purse on the side table and goes to get a drink. Her phone rings.

Captain Davis says, "I know this is a rugged time for you both but, hopefully, the circus will be over within a few days. My man is in place, so you can sleep soundly tonight."

"That's reassuring, sir. Thank you."

"You'll find the refrigerator is stocked, and you can call for food service whenever you like. I'll be in touch tomorrow morning, if not before."

"Thank you, Captain. Good night."

Trace stands close by, attempting to listen to the exchange. "What's up? What did he say?"

"He confirmed we're protected and don't need to worry about our security. He'll get back to us when he knows something, at least by tomorrow morning."

"That's reassuring."

"Did you check out the place? I want to show you the deck. The view's incredible."

Once outside, Lisa lowers her voice, "Something's not right."

Trace darts a look in each direction. He's learned to trust his sister's intuition. "Talk to me."

"Someone put a tracker on the car and might have bugged this suite. Before I picked you up, I pulled a device off the car's frame. I asked the captain about it. He explained that it's a GPS tracker and said it's for our protection. Standard procedure."

"Hmm, that seems logical."

"True, but in this last phone conversation, he said 'the circus will be over in a few days.' It might have been an innocent statement, but given your mention of a freak show, it made me wonder about his choice of words."

"Because you're not sure which side he's on?"

"Yes. I don't know whom to trust. And that concern includes my therapist."

"Therapist? Good grief, Lisa. Any more secrets you want to share?"

"Well … there's the matter of the dreams."

"Oh no. To use the captain's choice of words, this is enough of a macabre circus without adding dreams to it."

"Well, you asked."

"What about the therapist? Is this something new?"

"When I was arrested …"

"Wait a minute. *Arrested*?"

"Sort of. … When the murderer shot Dad and Mom, I called the police. It took them forever to respond. I got a little emotional because of that."

"And you accosted them?" Trace laughs. "I'll admit, you're scary when you get mad." He tries to control his amusement.

"Hey, it wasn't funny. Stop rolling your eyes. They put me in the back seat of a cruiser and took me to the station. Then the captain met with me and decided I wasn't a risk but was simply crazy. After he read the report, he assigned me to Dr. Schultz. I've met with him once."

"So, when's the next session?"

"Tuesday."

"That gives us some time. Remember my friend, Ryan?"

"Wavy blond hair?"

"I can't believe it. You had a crush on him, didn't you?"

Lisa turns away, trying to think of anything that might stop the flush creeping up her face, but she's caught. "I might have. I was just a kid. Remember, you're five years older than me."

"Well, you're not a kid now, and he's married—at least, he was the last time I spoke with him."

"Stop it." Lisa chuckles. "Why did you mention him?"

"He works for a big tech firm. He could sweep this place for bugs, and he might still live in the area and commute to New York City." At Lisa's interest, he adds, "I'll call him now."

Lisa returns to the suite and checks out the refrigerator. It's stocked with everything a person might need for a few days. The pantry holds an assortment of wine and bottles of vodka and dry vermouth. She smiles and decides what she will have later, then she wanders into the bathroom. Again, well equipped with organic shampoos and conditioners.

"Lisa?"

"Coming." She hurries to the deck.

"Ryan will stop by in about thirty minutes or so. Sound good to you?"

"Yeah. No problem at all. We can offer him a drink. We've got a stocked pantry."

"Nah, really?" He stands and goes over to the pantry and checks it out. "All right! I'm liking this holdup more and more. We can't let this go to waste. Ready for a drink?"

"Sure. I'll go with a cabernet."

At nine sharp, Ryan arrives, disheveled but dapper. As he enters the suite, he extends his arms as though he owns the world and laughs. "So, what's up, guys?"

Trace holds a finger to his lips in a warning to Ryan to watch what he says.

Ryan gets the message and turns playful. "Hey buddy, it's been years. You look fantastic. And who's this beauty? Lisa?"

"It's me."

"Wow, last time we met, you had pigtails and were excited about your new braces. It's hard to believe it's been that long ago." Ryan spins to look in all directions. "It had to have been Lisa who picked out this penthouse. It sure as heck wasn't you, my friend."

Trace laughs. "I won't even answer that. But let me show you around."

As they stroll around the suite, Ryan aims his detector at various angles, stops when he finds a mic, and motions to Trace.

Lisa tags along behind the two and, barely taking a moment to breathe, she explains why they're at the hotel. Ryan listens and side glances to Trace with raised eyebrows.

"It's for real." Trace grimaces.

Lisa continues, undeterred by their silent side glances. Without slowing, she tells Ryan about the police and the potential threat to their lives. When she takes a breath, Ryan suggests they move to the deck.

"We all need some fresh air." He smiles and offers a wink.

"Of course, of course. Great idea," Lisa says as her cheeks pinken.

Once outside, Ryan explains what he found. "I counted at least eight mics. Where's your purse, Lisa? We better check that as well." He follows her inside, inspects the purse, and gives her the okay sign. "This is nothing to laugh about. Eight mics are intense."

Lisa says, "I'm shocked there are *any* mics. I told Trace earlier that I don't know whom to trust, and this confirms my worst fears."

"Yeah, I'm glad you're here, buddy," Trace says. "We've got a lot to catch up on, but as you can tell, we're in the middle of a mess. And we need help. You were the first person to come to mind. The *only* person. Can you help?"

Ryan gives Trace an impish grin. "How could I pass it up? I've missed our shenanigans, and this one sounds like a doozy."

Trace smacks him a high-five. "Let's celebrate with a drink. I suspect we'll all need one—or three. We've got a wine cellar of everything from Cabs to Merlots, not to mention vodka and beer. Come with me, and you can choose your poison of choice."

A few minutes later, with drinks in hand, they go back outside on the deck, where they can talk freely.

"So, what's your assessment? You're the tech expert." Trace says.

"You've got a problem. Someone imagines you know more than you do, and they believe you're hiding that information. You're under constant surveillance, and I mean serious observation. Lisa, I suspect your car has mics as well. Do you want me to check it out?"

"Please. Earlier, I discovered a tracking device. I asked the police captain about it, and he claimed it helps them protect us."

Ryan shrugs and turns to Trace. "You and I could make a fast trip to the local liquor store. Might need more beer. You never know what the night will bring."

"Let's do it." Trace gets the keys from Lisa and leads the way out of the apartment.

As they drive away, Trace asks Ryan about his wife.

"How many years has it been, Trace? Six? That marriage lasted three years." While he talks, he moves his detector around the car. "I should have known, but the American Dream meant more to me than common sense." With his finger, he indicates another mic. "Yep, I thought I had it all for a few brief painful years."

"She seemed nice."

"Believe me, that was a smoke screen. How about you? Married? Kids?"

"Nope. Been too busy for either."

"And Lisa?"

"Single. Don't know if she's dating anyone, but she has a crush on you."

"Get out of here."

"I'm serious. I know my sister."

"Hmm."

They pull into the liquor store parking lot, and a black SUV lines up next to them. Trace risks a side glance. A heavyset, muscled man sits in the front seat. Plain-clothed police? Trace turns to Ryan and nudges him. "Six-pack?"

"Yep, that should do it."

"Can you stay a few more hours, like old times?"

"Of course. I wouldn't consider anything other."

They make quick work of purchasing beer, and when they get back to the hotel, Lisa sits on the deck, sipping wine. The black, starlit night frames her silhouette. She doesn't hear the door open or close and keeps listening to the late summer sounds of crickets chirping and frogs croaking in the distance. Her thoughts seem far, far away.

"Lisa," Trace says, startling her into the present. "Would you like a little more wine?"

"I'm fine for now."

Ryan ambles out with a drink in hand and runs his hand through his unruly mop. He resists the mirth that teases a smile and takes a seat near her.

"What are you listening to?"

"Just the night sounds. I find it comforting, don't you?"

"Hadn't thought about it much until you mentioned it. As a kid, I'd lay in the grass and watch the night sky. That's when I became aware of how different night sounds compared to the daytime—things like the hoots of a Great Horned Owl."

"Sometimes Trace would do the same thing, and I'd go out and join him. We'd stare into the abyss, and he'd point out the constellations and the shooting stars. It was a magical bonding time for us."

"It seems like centuries ago, doesn't it?"

"Uh-huh. We need more experiences like that."

Trace brings over some munchies and joins the two. "Just as we expected, there were mics in the car."

Lisa stares blankly at Trace and bites her lip. "I need more wine."

CHAPTER 6

Before sunrise, Lisa awakens gasping for air, and her heart pounds from a nightmare. In the dream, her father pushed her mother against a wall and threatened her with a choice, a heinous choice. Either she had to promise silence, or she'd never see her children again. Her mother begged on behalf of the kids. "I promise, I promise!" After that, Lisa woke up.

She fights the crumpled sheets and tosses the cover. *It's just a dream,* she tells herself. *It's just a dream. He wouldn't, would he?* Lisa stumbles out of the bed and walks to the bathroom. She steadies herself against the granite countertop, wipes the sweat off her forehead, and splashes chilly water on her face. Sick to her stomach, she leans over the sink, just in case. A glance into the mirror shows Lisa her mom, and she knows this was not *just a dream.*

Lisa darts back to the bed. She can't unsee what she's witnessed. A scream rises from her belly, which demands release. With a pillow clutched tight against her face, she heaves uncontrollably and lets loose an agonized screech. Now tumbling through time and space, she's a child, then an adult, and a child again. One morphs into the other until both become a blur. What she thought was her life was all fantasy.

As the horror of this realization sets in, Lisa glances over to the blinds on her bedroom window. Threads of light pour through—the beginning of another day. She takes a deep breath. *I can do this.* Her heartbeat calms, and the tears slow. *I'm not alone.*

A commotion of dishes clattering and cabinets opening and closing draws her attention to the suite. The familiar sounds of coffee percolating reach her along with its sumptuous aroma. Trace is awake.

Lisa slips into a hotel robe and joins him on the deck with a cup of morning brew.

"Sleep well?" He studies her response.

Lisa yawns and stretches. "Good enough, I guess. What's on the agenda today?"

"And that's the sidestep you're going to use with your big brother to avoid talking about your swollen red eyes?"

"I'm not ready to talk about it right now."

"Fair enough. So, my agenda? I suppose I should visit Dad's grave."

"Do you want to go there before we head to the hospital?"

"I don't want to visit at all, but it's a *should* I can't avoid," Trace says, tersely.

"Before we visit Mom, right?"

"Yeah. I need to get it over with. We can get breakfast after and then visit Mom."

"Do you ever wonder what she knows?"

"What brought that on?"

"Just thinking."

"She's not stupid. My guess is she's aware he was involved in shady deals. But I doubt she knows the details."

"My thoughts as well. He was gone most of the time. A few days a month were all he'd be home."

"Yeah, and our experience of those *few days* was vastly different. Dad would come into the house, and within minutes he'd be yelling at me. Then came the shoves and more. Not the same reception for you, now, was it, sis?"

"No." Lisa rubs her eyes. "I feared him, though. Once, I caught him peeking through my bedroom window while I dressed. After that, I never trusted him."

"Did you tell Mom?"

"I did, but it was a mistake. She talked to Dad and, well, you can guess the rest."

"What a mess. I cringe thinking about going to the cemetery, but I need to say a few choice words to Dad and have done with it. How much time do you need before we can leave?"

"I've had my coffee. Give me five minutes. I'll throw on some clothes and meet you at the door."

Trace nods and heads to the kitchenette to put the cups into the dishwasher and retrieves his baseball cap from the bedroom. Deep in thought, he looks out the window and clenches his jaw.

Lisa heads to the bedroom, and at his impatient "Are you ready?" she yells, "I'm coming, I'm coming." She dashes into the living room and snaps up her purse. "Let's face the traffic."

Minutes later, they maneuver onto the freeway, and within a short distance, they sit stuck in a deadlock.

"Commuter traffic," Trace moans. "This time of the day is challenging for drivers."

"You're worried about my driving, aren't you?"

"I didn't say that."

"You thought it." After a side glance, she smiles. "I've traveled this route to the cemetery a few times now."

"Just made a comment, that's all."

"Sure. You can't play innocent with me." She reaches and taps Trace's arm, pointing to the side-view mirror.

Trace looks in the mirror and nods. He makes a zipper sign across his lips.

The remainder of the drive passes in quiet contemplation, each of them locked in their thoughts.

Lisa brings the car to a stop and watches as the vehicle behind pulls over too.

Side-by-side, the siblings weave through the well-tended lawn, careful of the marble headstones, cement plaques, and granite statues. A funeral is in progress in the section across from them. Trace observes the mourners and rubs the side of his neck. *I'm glad I wasn't here for Dad's funeral. I'd rather make my peace now—alone except for Lisa.*

"Did you select the floral arrangement, Lisa?"

"Yeah. I remembered Mom saying that Dad liked red chrysanthemums and she has a special love for daisies. It was simple really. I just asked the florist to use those two flowers."

"You did well. Even though the spray's drying, some of the blossoms still linger. I can tell it was beautiful."

Lisa takes his hand. "Thank you."

"So, will you say a prayer or something? I'm only here to fulfill a societal duty. In my way of thinking, he doesn't deserve a visit by anyone."

"A prayer? Hmm. There are things I need to say to him. Maybe I can add a prayer as well." She draws closer to the freshly turned earth that covers the remains of her father.

"Dad, I don't know if I love or hate you, but I do know you destroyed our family. I pray to let go of you, let go of all that you once meant to me, and let go of all the insults, the twisted arms, the threats, the memories of seeing Mom's bruises, the memories of you hurling Trace against one wall and another, the memories of the baby, Robbie, who I'm certain you killed. Yes, today, I pray to let go of you. All of you. I pray to be washed clean of any thought of you. If you can hear me, and if you're not in the fires of hell, I pray you find your redemption by helping the family you destroyed. From the spirit world, find a way to redeem yourself, Dad. Give me one reason to love you, even if that reason is insignificant."

Trace looks at her with great compassion and chokes down his emotions. He rubs his hand across his face and clears his throat. Staring poker-faced at the mound, he says, "I can't do better than that, sis."

After taking an involuntary step back, Trace grimaces and finally offers his thoughts, "Dad, unlike Lisa, I *know* I hate you. You're the reason Mom is in the hospital. You're the reason we have a police escort everywhere we go. You're the reason our home is a crime scene. If Satan exists, you're one of his minions. Prove me wrong, Dad! Show me there's something redeemable about your life. Show you loved me, or anyone, other than yourself." With that, he grips a clot of earth and throws it forcefully onto the burial site.

He wipes away angry tears and shouts, "Let's get out of here."

Lisa takes Trace's hand and embraces him. He wraps his arms around her and cries in halting gasps. "It's not fair. It's not fair—what he did to our family and probably other families."

They return to the car and drive in silence to a nearby diner, both in deep thought. Once seated, they order breakfast and face each other. Lisa speaks first. "It's been an illusion, hasn't it?"

"What?"

"Our home life. An illusion of *all is well* while evil bedded down and entrapped us all."

Trace tilts his head and studies her. "I get what you're saying, but I haven't had enough coffee to get philosophical."

"That's just it. There's nothing philosophical about it. Last night I had a dream. It startled me awake."

Trace studies her intently. "Well?"

"In this dream, Dad threatened Mom. Either she remained silent about what she knew or suspected, or she would never see you and me again."

Trace stiffens, sits back, and runs his hand through his thick black hair. "You imagine this scenario is possible?"

Lisa bites her lower lip, looks down at the table, and back to Trace. "I believe it to be true."

Trace's eyes narrow as his indignation smolders. "I'll ask her today."

"She may not be able to answer."

"I'll know the answer one way or the other. She'll find a way to tell me."

"Maybe. You were her favorite."

"Not true. I'm the one she had to protect. Dad treated you differently than me. He considered me the intruder, the threat, and I wouldn't allow him to control me. At least, once I was big enough to fight, I didn't allow it."

Lisa lowers her head and twists the ends of her long curls. "I remember the attacks and his excuses. Invariably, he'd claim he had to discipline you because it was his responsibility. Otherwise, how would you learn right from wrong?" She looks over at her brother. "Ironic, don't you agree?"

Trace shifts in his seat and takes a swallow of water. "Enough of this rehashing. We'll get the answer today, and we can move on to other things."

"Like?"

"Like what did Dad have that these mobsters want?"

"Yep, my question as well. Of course, it begs another question. How did he get this mystery item in the first place?"

The server interrupts their conversation with their breakfast orders of eggs and bacon and a side of whole wheat toast. Trace thanks her and mentions the officer sitting two tables away. "Please, give me his tab. Whatever he orders, it's on me."

Trace glances at Lisa, who smiles. He shrugs. "It's the least I can do."

Thirty minutes later, they get into the car and head onto the freeway.

"Do you see the police lights ahead of us?"

"Yep. I'll take the next exit. I know a way to the hospital through the city streets. There's also a fire truck approaching from behind. There must be an accident. I'm moving over. If I can."

Trace purses his lips. "I've been watching our police detail, and I noticed there's another car following us as well."

"You sure?"

"Yep."

"Do you recognize it?"

"Not yet. White sedan. Female driver. That's all I can make out."

"Nothing surprises me anymore."

A traffic break opens ahead of them, and Lisa weaves through the traffic and clears the exit.

"Well done, sis."

"Did we lose our police officer?"

"Nope, he's right behind us. The white sedan's gone, though."

Lisa zigzags around the New Rochelle streets and drives into the hospital parking lot.

"You do know your way around."

Lisa grins and shakes her head. "I've made this drive at least twice a day for the past couple of weeks. I ought to know the area by now."

Lisa leads the way to the front-desk receptionist, who motions for them to proceed.

They step into the elevator, and Trace asks, "Two-eleven?"

"Correct. It's to our left as we exit."

When they near their mother's room, they hear laughter. Two nurse's aides share stories as they change the sheets and help Katherine get comfortable.

Trace crosses to the end of the bed and catches his mom's attention. "We'll talk in a little bit." She responds by lifting her hand.

A few minutes later, the aides leave, and Lisa and Trace sit at her side.

Trace takes his mom's hand. "We can tell you're feeling stronger, and nothing could make us happier."

She tries to smile, but only the right corner of her mouth curls upward.

Before Lisa can add her greeting, a nurse enters.

"It's good to see you both. I want you to know Katherine is recovering well. Every day there's a noticeable improvement. Tomorrow, the doctor will remove the stitches and do a full assessment."

Trace straightens. "Do you believe she'll be able to walk?"

"Yes. She has sensations in her legs and feet. Katherine may need a walker for a while, but in another week, she just might be able to go home. We're waiting for the neurological results. Hopefully, we'll have that tomorrow."

"I'm so relieved. This is the best news we've heard in a long while. Thank you."

"My pleasure. Enjoy the visit with your mom."

Lisa and Trace each hold one of their mother's hands. Together, they share about the improvements to the house, how it's getting repainted, and will be ready for her when she leaves the hospital. They tell her about Ryan's visit and the fun they had together.

As they talk, they watch as their mother tries to interact with a hand motion or a half-smile. Katherine whispers something, and the siblings draw closer. With measured speech, their mom says three words, "I love you."

The nurse enters the room and mentions they shouldn't stay much longer.

"We'll leave in a few minutes." Trace turns to his mother and strokes the side of her head. "I need to ask you something important." Without holding back, he asks, "Did Dad make you promise to keep silent about his work with threats he'd take Lisa and me away forever if you spoke?"

Katherine's eyes fill, and her face contorts. She looks at Trace imploringly and blinks through the tears. Her response is a whispered *YES*.

Unsuccessfully, Trace tries to hold back his tears. "No mother should ever face such a choice. You're safe now. He can't hurt you anymore." He leans and kisses her on the cheek. "We'll come back this evening."

Lisa makes her goodbyes, and she and Trace walk to the car in silence.

"You were right," Trace says. "As hard as Dad was with me, he imprisoned Mom. I won't leave until she's situated at home and Dad's mess is past tense."

Lisa blows her nose and wipes her eyes. "Thank you. I admit I'm overwhelmed, and having you at my side makes it more manageable." She gets behind the wheel, starts the engine, and backs out of the space.

Trace says, "When we get back to the hotel, I'll arrange for a month of vacation time. My work can wait. I'm needed here to tackle the unfinished business, and I'm not referring to the house. Dad was into something bad, and we need to find out what that was, so we can move forward with our lives."

"Do you still want to go to Mom's house before we head to the hotel?"

"Yeah. I want to check on things. Do you have the captain's number?"

"Yep. In my purse. Check the side pocket."

Trace finds it and makes the call. "Captain, this is Trace Holmes."

"Mr. Holmes. I'm sorry for your loss."

"Thanks. I'm calling to let you know our mother will be released next week, and we need to prepare the house for her return."

"So, she's making a good recovery?"

"That's right. She's doing better." Trace scowls while he listens to the captain.

"We can post officers inside the house for her protection once she's home."

Trace taps his fingers on the console. "No, the officers can rotate posts outside. I don't want them inside, beginning this weekend."

Lisa glances over at her brother and pulls over. His frustration is at a low boil. "As I stated, the cleanup needs to begin immediately. Your men can watch from a distance."

"You're aware of the extent of the damage and the ongoing threat?"

Trace hits the console. "I'm going there now to assess the damage. Captain, we've got to get on with our lives."

He ends the call and looks at Lisa. "I wouldn't leave now if the world turned upside down."

"He's not a bad guy, Trace. The man's following protocols and trying to get to the crux of the situation." Lisa rejoins traffic and, within minutes, she's at their mom's driveway, where she slams on the brakes. Multiple cars crowd the parking area. "Oh, my Lord. What else could go wrong?"

"Park by the curb. I'm going in."

"Not without me. I'm coming too."

Trace runs to the front door and shouts, "What's going on here?"

An officer confronts him, "This is a crime scene, sir. You need to leave."

"This is MY house. Who are these people? What are they doing?"

"It's not your business."

"Where's the search warrant? Without it, you better move fast and get out of my home."

A man in a suit joins them. "What's the trouble, officer?"

Trace says, "I've asked for a search warrant. This is my house. Why are you in it?"

The man flashes his FBI identification.

"I guess I should be impressed, Special Agent Travis, but I'm not. What the hell is going on?"

"I assume you're the son of the deceased."

"Well, that was tactful. Yes, I'm his only living son. I grew up here, and you didn't. So why are you here?"

"We have lingering questions."

"About?"

"About Mr. Holmes's connections."

"And they're hiding in the house?"

"Obviously not, but we might find leads."

"It's been over two weeks since Dad's murder. First, intruders ransacked the place, then the police came in and did their investigation. Now the FBI is here. I've yet to hear what everyone's looking for. The house is unlivable as it is, and no explanation is forthcoming. Surely you don't just go into random properties for no reason, do you?"

"We wouldn't be here if there wasn't cause."

"That's good to know. So, what's the cause?"

"I can't say."

"Of course not. But, Special Agent Travis, it's my right to see the search warrant."

"I don't have one."

Trace moves closer to the agent, and when face-to-face, he says, "I thought as much. Get your men out of here."

The agent glares at Trace for a while and, not breaking eye contact, shouts, "Jamison, Smith … get your men. We're leaving." To Trace, he says, "This isn't over." Travis pulls out a calling card and offers it to him. "Call me anytime."

After they leave, Trace looks at the police officers who remain. "Why are you here?"

"We were assigned."

Trace hits recall on his phone. "Captain, your men are standing in front of me. I'm putting you on speaker as I'm sure you want to say something to them."

The captain clears his throat. "Men, all shifts will be outside from this moment forward unless something unexpected comes up."

After the officers exit the building, Trace slams the door forcefully and shouts, "What crooked scheme was Dad involved in? Police, FBI, and soon we'll find out the CIA's part of the operation. Look at this place."

Lisa says, "I-I can't believe it. It's worse than when we first saw it." Randomly, she grasps one item and another and sets them back down. The house they once called home looks as though a tornado hit it. Wall hangings litter the floor, and large holes scar the walls. Couches lay upside down, gutted of their upholstery. Chairs lie scattered about the floor, some with broken legs. Even the pull stairway to the attic hangs loose.

She leans on Trace. "What will we do?"

Trace bites his lower lip and stiffens. While he surveys the damage, his eyes narrow. He kicks a broken chair and closes his fists. "We'll take photos of everything. This is our evidence."

He strides to the center of the room, where pry bars have lifted the floorboard and left a gaping hole. His lips tighten, and he spits out, "They must assume drugs or stashes of gold or dead bodies. Unbelievable."

Trace snaps photos. "Do you know Mom's insurance carrier?"

"When the washer flooded the basement, they contacted American Insurers. I'll search for the number now." Once she's found it, she shows Trace, and he makes the call.

Lisa wanders through the house while Trace talks with the insurance agent. When he's done, his sister stands by his side. "What did they say?"

"They're sending an assessor over tomorrow morning. I'll be here to meet with him. We'll have the house ready for Mom. I'll make sure of it."

"I'd go with you, but I have an appointment with the shrink."

CHAPTER 7

The following morning, Lisa knocks on Dr. Schultz's office door. He welcomes her in, but she says nothing. Instead, she hurries past him and takes a seat on the couch. He goes to his usual chair opposite his client.

Lisa stares out the window, arms crossed in front of her.

"I can tell you're upset. Please explain why."

"I don't know where to begin."

"So, it's been a difficult week. Start by telling me why."

Mockingly, she says, "Let's see, criminals ravaged my family home. The police and, separately, the FBI went through the house. They've torn open walls, pulled up floorboards, and shelves of books and treasures now adorn the floor. Should I go on?" She glares at the psychologist.

"You think I had something to do with that?"

"The police recommended you."

"And a recommendation means I work for them?"

"There are thousands of shrinks in this area, so why'd they pick you?"

"They know me from prior cases. Also, I work with several officers who suffer from PTSD." He crosses his arms and narrows his focus on Lisa. "So, you don't trust me, right? That's why you're resistant to coming here. Let's start with that and talk about why you feel suspicious of me."

"Fine. Tell me what's going on. No one else will. Our family home looks like wreckage from a warzone. There's no search warrant, no explanation, and no simple, *I'm sorry*."

"You may not believe this, but I didn't know this was going on and have no idea why they've destroyed your home. However, I do understand your mistrust of me. If I were in your shoes, I wouldn't trust me either."

"At least we agree on that point."

"You and I are on a journey together. It may lead to the answers you seek. Because of that, we need to persist. If you feel otherwise, we'll go our separate ways. You decide. I'm here for you, not the other way around. What do you want?"

Lisa rubs her fingers on her lower lip and studies the floor. After a long pause, she says, "If we proceed, I need to know you're on my side, and words themselves won't convince me."

"That's fair. When I work with a client, I accompany them into their personal terror. I feel it. I know it. It's a sacred space for me."

Lisa scowls and taunts him, "Why *sacred*?"

"When we share common space, there's no separation. As I honor you, I honor myself."

Lisa considers his response and shakes her head. "You know what, for the last several weeks I've lived with horror. It's not something sacred. It destroys all that's good. I understand what you're trying to say, and the best I can do is meet you in the middle. I will work with you, but my questions remain. Time will resolve or confirm my doubts. Nothing else."

Schultz puckers his lips and nods. "Okay. In the middle, it is. A cautious truce?"

Lisa gives him a quick salute.

The psychologist sits back in his overstuffed chair. "You know the process. The first step is to move into an altered state. Please, take several deep breaths and allow yourself to fade into the silence."

He taps his foot rhythmically and quietly until Lisa relaxes. Softly and in a measured cadence, he guides Lisa's thoughts, "You're at your father's funeral. Your mom sits beside you, but she's unable to move. You drift upwards, and from this higher perch, you look at all the visitors. You recognize a few neighbors, but otherwise, you don't know most of the attendees. Let your vision travel from one mourner to the next. When you spot someone who triggers a memory, signal with your hand."

Uncomfortable, Lisa squirms in her seat.

Schultz says, "Is the person you're looking at a man or a woman?"

"Woman."

"Where have you seen her before?"

"She spent a few nights at our house."

"How long ago?"

"I was just a kid, but some people you never forget."

"From your expression, you didn't like her."

"Not one bit. I felt scared around her. She'd undress in front of my brother and me when my parents were out of the house."

"Did she touch you?"

"No. I told Mom what she did, and she got angry at her, and the woman left."

"What about your father? What did he say?"

"He pooh-poohed it. She was his friend."

"How did they become friends?"

"I don't know. Dad told us he met her at a museum."

"So, he invited a stranger to your house?"

"That's what he claimed."

"And your mother was okay with this?"

"She accepted it but didn't like it."

"Are you still looking at the woman?"

"Yes."

"What's she doing?"

"Texting someone. I remember now. Her name's Elena."

Schultz shifts in his seat. "Is anyone with her?"

"Yes. A man. I've seen him too. He visited my father outside in our yard on two occasions."

"Do you know who he is?"

"Dad only commented that he owned a big department store in NYC."

"And he drove out to New Rochelle to meet with your father in your yard?"

"Yes. He rode in a limousine."

"What's the man doing?"

"Looking at someone."

"Describe the person he's looking at."

"He's got a cap pulled down low. He fidgets a lot. He signals the man from the limousine."

"What kind of signal?"

"He moves his finger and then points."

"Follow his finger. On whom is he focused?"

Lisa straightens and wrings her hands.

"You've seen him before?"

"He's the one who killed my father. I'm sure of it." Lisa puts her hand over her mouth and uncrosses her legs. "I don't want to do this anymore."

"Just a few more minutes. At whom is that man looking?"

"My mother. I have the impression he's trying to decide if she's alert."

"Does he concentrate on you?"

"Only briefly. He's interested in my mom."

"Let yourself float higher above the crowd. What catches your attention?"

Lisa wraps her arms around herself. "These people are working together. There's something they want, and they're dangerous."

"Okay, let yourself float back into your chair and take several long breaths."

Once Lisa feels comfortable and can breathe normally, Schultz asks, "How're you doing?'

"I worry about my mom. They think she knows something or has something. Whatever it is, they want it. They'll come back."

"Do you believe your mother knows something?"

"I doubt it. Dad was unbelievably secretive, and she had nothing to do with his work."

"When do you imagine she'll be released to go home?"

"The doctor said maybe next week."

"Hmm. When will you return to the house?"

"Before Mom gets released."

"You'll need protection. You know that, right?"

"Yeah."

"I'll share something few people know. My wife was murdered because she ended up in the wrong place at the wrong time. While walking down a street, she heard a child scream and followed the sounds. Innocently, she got caught in a drug exchange. When the police got there, they thought she was involved. She wasn't. But it was this situation that led to me doing the work I do now. This is my way of helping people through the grief process."

Lisa's mouth drops open. "Who killed your wife?"

"To this day, I don't know who shot her. The police? The criminals? It doesn't matter because the result is the same. But this is why I help anyone who faces what I had to eight years ago."

"And you've found peace through it all?"

"Peace is a strong word. I've found healing, which is why I promised it to you. I know how to let go. Now, did you do the assignment I gave you?"

"Yes and no."

"Explain."

"I paged through the book and selected those images of facial parts that resembled the killer, but I couldn't put the pieces together."

"Because you were afraid of what you'd find."

"Because I didn't want to face him. The murderer."

"What about now?"

"I'm ready."

Together, Lisa and Dr. Schultz create the image of the gunman through a patchwork of images. Lisa looks long and hard at the finished puzzle.

"Confused?"

"No. I'm wondering why. The composite is the man I saw at the funeral. He's the killer. But how will we identify him?"

"I have friends in high places. They do favors for me, and I do favors for them. Give me a minute while I fax Jeanne the image."

A text confirmation rings in. "Okay, she's running it through facial recognition as we speak."

"Thank you."

"I also asked you to write down thoughts, memories, and dreams. Anything out of the ordinary. Did you do so?"

"I did, but there's not much to share, except for one dream."

"Are you willing to share it with me?"

"Yeah. In the dream, my father threatened my mother. He made her promise she would never speak about anything related to what he was doing. If she did, he would take my brother and me away, and she'd never see us again."

"Did she promise? In your dream?"

"Yes. And today, at the hospital, Trace asked her, and Mom acknowledged it as truth. The dream was accurate."

"How does that make you feel?"

Lisa studies Schultz. "How would it make you feel, doctor?" Her lips tighten, and her stare narrows. "I'm confused by it all. I'm no longer shocked by the insanity around me. I expect it. How pathetic is that? I'm left wondering if my entire childhood was a lie. At the same time, I also understand some things now—especially why my mom would never question or confront him."

"He knew how to control your mother."

"Not just her. All of us."

A text message interrupts the session. Schultz reads it and says, "Jeanne has identified the composite photo as Joseph Gagnon. Ever heard of him?"

"Never."

"Well, I'll ask my friend to search for employment records, police records, anything." He texts out a quick message and turns back to Lisa. "This may take a while, but she'll be in touch soon. This is a good place to stop for the day. When I receive an update from Jeanne, I'll let you know."

"Thank you." Lisa reaches for her purse and stands.

"Before you leave, I've another assignment. But before I get to that, I want to underscore that you need to take every precaution. From all you've told me, you're in danger. It's good you're staying in the hotel and not at the house. They'll come after you, so make certain you have protection. As for the assignment, I want you to pay attention to odd things—synchronicities, strange items, or words. Things that seem out of place or just odd. Will you do that?"

"Yeah."

"On both counts?"

"I'll try."

"*Try* isn't good enough. It will get you killed—then what have you achieved? You must make certain you stay as safe as possible."

"I will."

"Okay, then, I'll see you next week."

Lisa makes her way down the hallway to the elevator. She listens as the door closes to Schultz's office and turns to make sure he's not standing there, watching. *Why don't I trust him? He says the right things, but I still have this uneasy feeling he's using me.*

When the elevator door opens, Lisa walks into the enclosure and adjusts her crossbody bag. She stands to the side of a young man, who nods to the beat of the *Black-Eyed Peas.* The music plays loudly enough for Lisa to hear it through his earbuds. An older woman stands at the back of the elevator. She gives Lisa a look that says, *Can you believe it?* Lisa smiles and shrugs.

At her car, Lisa drops into the driver's seat and rests her head on the steering wheel. When she checks her rearview mirror, she spots the protective security detail. *It's for the best.* She sinks into her seat and catches a glimpse of someone who looks like Gagnon. Intrigued, Lisa leans closer to the window. It is. Joseph Gagnon. *What's he doing here?* She squints her eyes to be sure. *Yes, it's the man who killed Dad.*

Alarmed and terrified, Lisa stares as the murderer disappears into the office complex she exited moments ago. Without a thought about her safety, and needing to know, Lisa hurries out of the car and follows the man. He disappears into the elevator, and she watches the indicator panel, which stops on the second floor—Schultz's floor. Lisa runs up the stairs and sees Gagnon talking to Schultz. They argue, and Schultz tries to close the door. Gagnon brandishes a handgun, and all goes silent after the crack of the gun fire. With a single bullet, Schultz falls.

Gagnon races down the staircase at the end of the hallway while Lisa runs to Schultz.

"No, no, no!" Lisa calls 911 immediately and kneels beside her therapist. She attempts to slow the blood that gushes from his shoulder and screams for help from anyone who might hear. *How can this be happening—again?*

The security detail comes to Lisa's aid at the same time the EMTs arrive. She cries hysterically and stares at her hands, covered in Schultz's blood. The undercover officer guides Lisa away from the scene while the rescuers administer immediate care and rush Schultz to the ambulance.

Lisa watches and looks at the officer pleadingly. "Will he be okay?"

"I don't know, ma'am, but when I do, I'll let you know. Are you able to drive? I can give you a ride back to the hotel."

She assures him she can drive herself. And, behind the wheel again, she starts the car and backs out. Tears flood her vision. The car hits the curb hard and startles her.

The officer blocks her vehicle. "Ma'am, I'm driving you to the hotel. It's not safe for you to handle an automobile right now. Please, get in the back seat."

He opens the patrol car door and waits for her to enter. Once she's seated, the officer takes her keys and parks her car in a slot before driving back to the hotel.

Lisa wraps her arms around herself, as a bone-deep chill races up and down her body. She shivers while she weeps. A police dispatch sounds over the radio, "Gunshot victim en route to Mercy Hospital. Blue SUV, NY plate King-Lincoln-Victor-7837 last spotted on Carter St. Officers in pursuit." The officer glances through the rearview mirror and tells Lisa not to worry. "We'll get him."

At the hotel, the officer drapes a blanket around Lisa and guides her into the back elevator and up to her suite. He rings the doorbell. "You'll feel better soon, ma'am."

Trace answers the door, and his eyes widen. "What happened? Are you okay?"

"She is fine, sir. Scared but not hurt physically. I put a blanket around her because she's got blood all over her. Here are her keys. I wouldn't let her drive."

"Thank you, officer. What happened?" Trace pulls Lisa close to him and holds her tight against his chest.

"There was a shooting, sir, but Ms. Holmes wasn't involved. She was a witness and tried to help the victim. Which is why she has blood on her clothes."

"Thank you for your help, officer. I'll handle it now." Trace pockets the keys, helps Lisa into the room, and closes the door.

Ashen, Lisa shakes uncontrollably. "I'm cold … cold." Her lips tremble.

Trace tightens the blanket around her. "Take a deep breath, sis. I'm with you. It will be okay." He guides her to the bathroom. All the while Lisa mutters incoherent words, not sentences, and stares at her bloodied hands.

He opens the shower door and turns the handle to *hot*. "This will warm you up. We'll talk after. I want to know exactly what happened. I'm just a few steps away, so if you feel weak or get scared, you call out. Got it?"

"Yes."

Trace walks back to the main room and paces, his thoughts racing. *She met with the psychologist. Something happened there.* He takes hold of his phone and taps out a text. After shoving the phone into his pocket, Trace slams the back of the couch with his closed fist. Lisa takes a quick shower, evidently too jittery to enjoy the hot spray. She comes out wrapped in a towel, her brunette curls dripping onto the floor.

Trace turns and faces her. "I know you're comfy, sis, but you better get dressed because Ryan will be here soon."

"Why didn't you tell me?"

"I just did."

Lisa hurries into her bedroom.

Trace walks the perimeter of the room, deep in thought. Tapping sounds at the door. An eye to the peephole, he sees the police officer from earlier. Trace opens up. "How can I help, officer?"

"I wanted to make sure Lisa is okay. If you need help, I'm here."

"Thank you. She's in the shower right now and told me she doesn't want to talk with anyone. If something comes up, I'll let you know immediately."

"When she's ready, I need to speak with her about what she saw. It won't take long."

"I understand completely and will be in touch. Thank you." Trace closes the door and rests his back against it. His shoulders fall and his thoughts race about Lisa. *If something happens to her, I'll never forgive myself.*

Trace walks back and forth across the room and out to the deck. He hasn't prayed for years, but in his desolation, his childhood prayer to his guardian angel comes to mind. *I can't lose Lisa. I simply can't.* He whispers the prayer he said often when he felt afraid and wipes away his tears.

More knocking comes at the suite's main door, and Trace strides over to check. Ryan has arrived. Trace opens the door and motions for his friend to enter.

"What's going on?"

Trace looks up at the ceiling to remind Ryan of the mics. "How about a coke?"

"Sounds good. Deck?"

"Yeah. I'll be right with you." Trace takes a couple of cans from the refrigerator and steps outside.

"Well?"

"Lisa went to her therapy appointment and returned covered in blood. She wasn't hurt, but she's in shock. Shaking. Cold. She'll be out here soon—just getting dressed after her shower. The security detail drove her back here and told me she witnessed a shooting and ran to help the victim."

"You can't make this stuff up. I'm sorry, man."

"Scared the hell out of me. I don't know what I'd do if something happened to Lisa. When things settle here, we'll need to pick up her car."

"Not a problem. The real issue is growing more complicated and dangerous by the day. I'll use some of my vacation time to work with you. Remember when we were kids? We thought we were detectives. It's time we make that childhood game real."

"Thank you. That's a relief to hear."

Lisa walks over, carrying a glass of iced tea.

Ryan watches while Lisa takes a seat. "What's going on?"

Lisa stares at her brother and Ryan. "I'm not sure, but there are a few things I do know. Joseph Gagnon shot my psychologist. He's the man who killed Dad and hurt Mom."

"You sure?"

"I saw him fire the weapon. I was down the hall."

"Did you say anything to the police?"

"No, but the detail arrived soon afterward."

Trace shifts uncomfortably. "You didn't talk with them because you wonder if they're involved."

"Exactly."

The trio moves their chairs closer and huddles in to hear Lisa's story. She tells them about the exercise and the photo compilation and explains how one of the psychologist's associates identified Gagnon and is now digging into his past.

"We finished our work for today's session, and I went to the car. Because I felt upset, I sat there for a few minutes and tried to process the session. I saw Gagnon walking into the building and thought he might be conspiring with the shrink, so I followed. He knocked on the door, and Dr. Schultz opened it. Schultz yelled something like, 'No. Leave!' And I watched him try to close the door. Gagnon shot him and ran. It was horrifying."

Trace reaches out and puts his hand on Lisa's shoulder.

"I called nine-one-one and sat with Dr. Schultz until they came. I put my hands over his wound and applied pressure. That's when I got his blood on me. I wanted to go to the hospital, but I was a mess, and the officer moved me away from the scene."

Trace says, "It's good you came back."

"When we go to the hospital to see Mom, I want to check on Schultz. I'm ashamed I doubted him."

Ryan reaches for his phone. "Do you want me to do an electronic search on this guy, Gagnon?"

"Please."

Ryan pulls out his cell and starts a search.

Trace asks, "Is there anything else? Any other connections?"

Lisa looks at her brother intently. "There's a group of them. Four or five. I saw them at the funeral. They seemed focused on Mom."

"And now you."

"Maybe."

"There's no *maybe*. It's for sure. So, who were these guys?"

"Not just *guys*. Remember Elena? She stayed with us a couple of nights when we were kids. She and Dad were tight."

"I can't forget her, as much as I'd like to."

"She's part of that group."

"And the others?"

"Besides Joe Gagnon, do you remember the guy who came out to our house in a limo and talked with Dad outside by the maple tree?"

Trace grimaces and nods.

"He sat next to Elena at the service. Fidgeted the whole time."

"I remember him. A New York City billionaire, per Dad. What person drives an hour or more, visits a nobody for ten minutes, and leaves?"

"Exactly."

"Hey, you two, sorry to interrupt, but I found something. Gagnon has quite a history. The military booted him for disorderly conduct, then he spent time in Sing Sing, and he's held multiple security positions with major businesses. I could go on. Frankly, his background fits that of a hitman."

Trace pushes back into his chair and runs a hand through his hair. "What have we gotten ourselves into? We're dealing with criminals, but we don't know why, and we don't know who's behind it all."

Lisa takes a slow swallow of iced tea. "How do you feel about the police?"

"Short answer, something's fishy. As for the guy across the hall, he's just doing his job."

"Yeah, my thoughts on both counts."

Ryan says, "Your theory doesn't explain the FBI's involvement. Why did they get mixed up in this? And who called them? Or did anyone call them? I'm the outsider to this craziness, but I suspect the FBI has trailed your dad for years. Who knows, maybe he worked with them. Anyway, I tend to think the police, or at least the men on the ground, are average dudes doing what they're assigned to do."

Trace nods in agreement. "I can accept that, even agree with you, but someone is relaying information to the FBI. There's an inside person. And, considering the risks and uncertainty, I believe we should stay underground as much as possible. When we go to visit Mom, we'll take your car, Lisa. But if we decide to do our own police work, let's use Ryan's."

Ryan nods. "Agreed. But, earlier, you told me Lisa's car is parked near the therapist's office."

"You're right. We need to collect it. Shall we do that now?"

"I'm ready."

CHAPTER 8

Late in the afternoon, the self-proclaimed detectives arrive at the hospital. Lisa carries a planter of daisies but struggles with the revolving hospital doors.

"Over here, Lisa." Ryan holds open a side entrance.

"Thank you. I didn't consider the doors when I bought this live arrangement. My focus was on making Mom happy."

"You'll do that for sure. It's beautiful."

Trace walks to the reception desk and picks up the visitor passes.

"You know what, guys," Ryan says. "How about you two spend quality time with your mom, and I'll catch up with my messages down here in the waiting room."

"You're sure?"

"Absolutely."

As Trace and Lisa walk to the elevator, Ryan grabs one of the nearby black scoop chairs and slides onto it. After rolling his neck, he checks out the room and finds the usual tattered magazines, a water cooler in the corner—but with no cups—a wall-mounted television with images but no sound, and five or six people texting on their phones. A little boy, who sits on the floor pushing a small green truck, distracts Ryan. He smiles at the sounds the child creates and remembers doing the same at that age.

The boy moves his toy truck across the floor and, accidentally, touches the shoes of a woman seated near the doorway. Ryan's eyes meet hers, and she responds by raising a newspaper in front of her face and uses one hand to text a message.

Ryan reaches for a magazine and flips through the pages while staying alert to sudden movements. A man matching Joe Gagnon's description walks into the room and nods to the mystery woman. Ryan watches as the guy sits three seats from her and darts a look at Ryan. When the man puts his hand over his pocket, Ryan tenses and considers what Lisa shared earlier.

The front-desk receptionist announces, "Mr. Nicolas Lopez, you can enter now."

Ryan makes a run for it. "Coming." He springs out of his seat and moves to the receptionist to claim the Lopez visitor's card.

Gagnon rises out of his seat, but the woman signals for him to sit.

Ryan takes the visitor's card and disappears into the elevator. At the second floor, he exits and spots Trace.

"Hey, we have a problem."

Trace meets him midway. "What's going on?"

"Gagnon's downstairs, and I'm certain he'll be getting off the elevator in a few. Is the shrink on this floor as well?"

"No, he's still in the ER. The nurse just told us his condition is *good*. See the police officer at the end of the hall? He's on watch along with the officer at Mom's door."

"We've got to alert both. There's going to be action."

Lisa comes out of the room. "What's happening?"

"I just saw Gagnon downstairs, and I believe he's armed."

Lisa covers her mouth. "He's coming after Mom."

"And you."

Trace takes hold of Lisa's arm. "Get back inside the room."

Ryan shouts to the police guards, "An armed man is coming up the elevator. Ready yourselves."

Along with Ryan, Trace ducks into Katherine's room and locks the door. They stand beside the exit and listen while shots sound in the hallway. Then they hear, "Officer down, officer down!"

Trace cracks open the door. An officer lies on the tile flooring. Gagnon takes aim at the other uniformed man. The police officer fires before Gagnon and knocks him flat.

"Assassin down. Where's my backup?" the officer radios. With his gun pointed at Gagnon, he moves forward. "Looks like a clean hit. No sign of life." Cautiously, a nurse walks out of a patient's room. She bends to check the assassin's vitals and declares him dead.

At the other end of the hall, another officer appears and rushes to assist. He goes straight to the hit officer. "We're going to help you, buddy." He yells down the hallway, "We need medical attention down here."

A nurse hurries to his side and kneels beside the officer. "Sir, look at me. I'm going to help you. You're shot. A doctor is on the way."

The officer mutters a few words. "My side … hurts."

"Yes, I'm applying pressure until the doctor arrives. You'll be okay. Stay with me."

A doctor dashes out of the elevator.

"Over here," the nurse shouts. "This officer has a gunshot wound."

The doctor makes a quick assessment and calls for a gurney. "Sir, I'm taking you to surgery. We need to repair the damage and close your wound. Do you understand?"

"Yes." The officer's response is barely audible.

As the medical team moves to the elevator, three police officers exit and speak to their injured friend. "Hang in there, partner. We're with you."

Ryan hurries to the police officers. "There's another person in the waiting room. A female. The shooter and she are in this together." He offers a description, and one of the officers calls for hospital security and runs down the stairs.

The elevator opens again. An aide pushes a gurney to a room down the hall. Lisa watches as the aide stops at Dr. Schultz's assigned quarters. When the aide leaves, she peers inside and enters.

"Lisa?"

"Yes. I'm visiting my mother and saw that you're on the same floor. I wanted to say I'm so sorry, Dr. Schultz. This is my fault, isn't it?"

"Of course not. Someone bugged my phone. Why all the police?"

"Gagnon came here and shot a police officer."

"Unbelievable. First me and now a police officer?"

"A nurse just declared the shooter dead."

"That's a relief. One down."

Lightly, Lisa touches Schultz's hand. "I feel awful I ever doubted you. Will you be okay?"

"Absolutely. I won't visit the gym for a while, but give me a few weeks, and I'll be as good as new."

"When can you go home?"

"They haven't said, but I assume within a few days."

A nurse walks in and motions to Lisa that she needs to leave.

"It looks like I have to go, but I'll stop by tomorrow when I visit my mother."

"When you come, you can update me on your homework."

"For real?"

"For real."

Lisa grins. "Done."

Lisa returns to her mom's room to find Dr. Rodriguez and Trace at Katherine's bedside. Ryan stands by the window and appears deep in thought.

The doctor takes Katherine's hand. "After the chaos we just experienced, I thought it a perfect time to share some great news. Your injury is challenging because of the nearness to the brachial plexus, but the nerves don't appear damaged. Any movement limitation is, probably, the result of swelling around the trauma itself. With proper care and follow-up from physical therapy, I believe your neurological deficits will resolve within a few weeks, a month at most."

"Does this mean she'll be able to talk?"

"Yes. I have no doubts about that. I've arranged for a speech therapist to meet with Mrs. Holmes later this afternoon. The therapist will perform an assessment and create a care plan. I'm confident you'll see daily improvement."

Trace turns away, wipes tears from his cheeks, and bends over his mom to kiss her forehead.

Lisa stretches and enfolds her arms around Katherine. "You'll be okay, Mom. You're going to be okay."

Tears run down Katherine's face, and she whispers *thank you* to Dr. Rodriguez.

"It's been a pleasure, my dear. I wish all my cases had a similar hopeful outcome. I'll check in with you tomorrow." She leaves with a wave to all.

A moment later, shouting down the hospital hallway interrupts the tender sentiments.

Ryan darts to the doorway and watches the police action. After a moment, he turns back to the others. "There's no threat. The police are organizing themselves."

A female yells, "Check everyone's ID as they step off this elevator. Williams, don't move from this site. Understood?"

Another assignment reaches their ears, "Harris and Sanchez, you cover the stairs. This thug reports to someone. We're going to find the monster."

Ryan says, "I suspect you'll hear commotion for a while, but that's good. You're protected, so don't worry about anything."

Trace tells his mom, "We'll come back in the morning. When we leave, I'll close the door. It will be quieter then. Can I get anything for you?"

Katherine smiles, shakes her head slowly, and motions for her son to draw near. She whispers, "I'm happy."

Trace's eyes tear. "I am too."

CHAPTER 9

Trace, Lisa, and Ryan weave their way through the police, medical staff, and investigators who crowd the hallway. When they reach the ground floor, they check the waiting room. The mystery woman isn't there.

"Can you describe her, Ryan?" Lisa asks.

"Sort of. Light brown hair, dark eyes, aging skin. I'd guess her to be around sixty years old."

"You probably saw Elena."

Trace says, "Did you notice anything unusual about her fingers?"

"Come to think of it, yes. She held a newspaper to cover her face, so her hands were visible. The little finger caught my attention because it's only a stump."

"That's Elena. Well, sis, you called it right. We're dealing with an organized ring. The question is why? How was Dad tied to these mobsters?"

Lisa stops in front of the car. "Can one of you drive? I'd rather sit in the back—I need to calm down."

Trace takes her keys, and Ryan hops in the front with him.

"Do you still want to stop at the house before returning to the hotel, Lisa?"

"Yes."

"All right. Next stop, the house. I'd like to check on the repair progress."

Ryan looks over at Trace. "Insurance is covering the repairs?"

"Yeah. Fortunately, they've agreed to cover all the costs. The damage to the house and the replacement of the furniture."

Lisa rests her head against the door frame and drifts into a twilight state. She revisits her childhood experiences with Elena and her dad. She sees how Elena flirts with him and draws him away from the family. Watches how she controls him and, in turn, her mother. Suddenly, she remembers the hiding place, where her dad would leave her candy and, sometimes, little figurines.

When they pull into the driveway, police officers stand in the front yard, smoking.

Lisa says, "Could you guys occupy the officers for a few minutes? I want to wander through the house alone. I need to figure something out. Just give me five minutes."

Trace looks at Ryan. They both shrug and amble over to the police.

Lisa enters through the front door, dashes through the house, and exits out the back. Furtively, she glances in all directions to make certain she's alone. When she locates the tall oak tree she used to climb as a kid, she dashes over to it. Just as she remembers, there's a knot hole midway up the trunk. Lisa stretches, and with her middle finger, searches for hidden objects. She finds no candy, no little figurine, but there is something else—a key. She pockets it and hurries back into the house just as Trace and Ryan enter through the front door.

"Bro, I found something." Lisa reaches into her pocket and pulls out the key.

"What's it to?"

"I don't know."

"Where did you get it?"

"Well, that's a bit of a story, but I found it in the oak tree."

"You're kidding."

"Nope. How about I explain once we're back at the hotel."

"Yeah, with a drink in hand. By the way, the cops told me there was a crew here today working on the walls. They'll be back tomorrow. It's a slow process, but the work has begun."

"It'll be a long time before this house feels like a home again."

"True. But I'll make sure Mom has a home to return to. You ready to go?"

"Yep."

Back at the hotel, Ryan calls out to Lisa, "Would you like a glass of wine?"

"Yeah, make it a tall one."

"Now we're talking. I'm having vodka. If I could, I'd take it intravenously. It's been one of those days."

Trace laughs. "I'm with you, buddy. I'd take it by IV as well, but I'll settle for a stiff drink."

Lisa tosses her purse on the sofa and strolls out to the deck, where she inhales deeply and looks out at the flickering city lights. A hawk dips and rises and disappears. Lisa takes a slow inhalation.

While smiling at the kitchen playfulness and the pop of a cork, Lisa turns and selects her seat. She can't help but chuckle as memories of their high school years come to mind. They had the reputation of being the life of the party.

Ryan takes a seat next to hers and raises his glass. "Let's toast. To surviving another day with the Holmes kids. I haven't had this much excitement since getting deposed for my divorce. Hear, hear!"

Trace and Lisa laugh at his antics.

Ryan says, "It's good to hear you two laugh about the day. Life's too short, and I don't want death to settle in with us."

After the celebratory first swallow, Lisa clears her throat. "I want to follow up on a conversation I had with Trace at the house."

Ryan glances at his buddy and tilts his head playfully, pretending to be annoyed. "I suspect this will be a long night."

Lisa sips her wine. "I'll start from the beginning. When we left the hospital, I remembered Dad used to play a game with me when I was little. Occasionally, he'd hide candy in a knot hole in the old oak tree in the backyard. I'd climb on its limbs and search that hole for treasures. While you two talked to the police, I went out to the tree. I could barely reach the knot hole, but to my surprise, there was something in it."

"Well?"

"As I mentioned to Trace, I found a key."

Ryan side-glances at Trace.

Lisa pulls the key from her jeans pocket and shows them.

Trace asks, "And you don't know what it goes to?"

"Correct. But I do know Dad wouldn't have put it there if he didn't want me to find it."

Ryan teases, "How much wine have you had?"

"Come on, I'm serious. But to your question, not enough." For emphasis, Lisa takes a couple more swallows. "Better."

"This is all a bit weird to me, but what the heck." Ryan fingers the key. "It's four-sided, so probably a house key. Did your dad have a girlfriend?"

At their sour expressions, he raises his eyebrows. "Sorry, I take that back. Too intrusive."

Lisa says, "Not really. It's something we should consider. He's had, umm, *acquaintances* over the years."

"Along those lines, did he have a secret office or a mountain escape?"

"He could have had both, for all I know," Trace says.

Lisa stays silent and gulps down the rest of her wine. Both Ryan and Trace focus on her. Trace says, "What's going on? What do you know?"

"I need more wine."

Ryan stands and fetches the bottle. "To the top?"

She salutes a *yes*.

"Lisa, you haven't answered my questions."

She exhales and begins her confession, "I remember a cabin in the woods. I was just a little kid. I remember holding my Cabbage Patch doll, Priscilla. This could be my imagination playing tricks on me, but I can only remember being there one time. It was dark and scary. Dad made me stay in the car, but I didn't like being alone. I called out to him, but he didn't respond, so I climbed out of the car. I remember stumbling on a rocky path to the cabin and looking in a window. I saw him with a stack of money. He was yelling about something and threw papers into the fireplace. I got chills and ran back to the car.

"When he came out of the cabin, he put something under a big rock at the side of the house. I saw him coming toward the car, so I laid down in the seat and pretended to be asleep. After he'd driven for a while, I opened my eyes and stretched. He noticed me and asked if I'd had a good nap. I said yes and asked if the cabin was a secret place. He said it was and it was our special secret, and no one else should ever know."

Trace and Ryan look, fixedly, at Lisa. Finally, Trace says, "What the hell? Why didn't you say something?"

"I only remembered today when I found the key. Dad used to say the knot hole was our secret hiding place, and today the word *secret* triggered my memory."

"Do you know the location of the cabin?"

"I might. Somehow, I know Priscilla is important. Maybe there's a Priscilla road or street."

Ryan grabs his smartphone and makes an online search.

Trace watches Ryan. "Check the tri-state area. You might have more luck."

Within minutes, Ryan shouts, "Got it. There's a Priscilla Court and a Priscilla Road in New Jersey. There's a Priscilla Place in ..."

"That's it, that's it," Lisa shouts. "I remember Dad saying, 'This is your dolly's special place. Priscilla's Place.'"

Trace nods and taps at his phone screen. "Okay then. Priscilla's Place is in Putnam Valley. That's a wooded area. I'll check for local photos."

"I don't recall any houses around the cabin but remember lots of trees. It was getting dark when we were there, and I couldn't see any lights."

"Why were you with him?"

"I don't know. But I didn't feel like he wanted me with him. It could be that Mom was in the hospital with Robbie, and he had to take care of me."

Trace shrugs. "That makes sense. I would have been at school or soccer practice." Trace looks from one to the other. "You know what we must do."

Lisa nods.

"Yep," Ryan says. "It's going to take some planning, but I have an idea that might work."

CHAPTER 10

At four o'clock the following morning, with the half-moon visible through the pine trees, Trace and Lisa prepare for a trip. The sun won't rise for another two hours, and they plan to be at their destination by daybreak.

Not saying a word, the pair scurry around the suite. As planned, they program the TV to play at half past seven and the coffee maker to begin brewing at the same time. They re-check the backpack for the area map, extra clothes, bottles of water, and a few energy bars. At the door, Lisa takes her briefcase *just in case.* They're ready to go. With a quick high-five, the two sneak down the stairs to the first floor. Upon seeing no one, they exit to the back of the hotel.

In the rental jeep, the lack of light makes Ryan barely visible. Lisa and Trace load their gear in the cargo area and climb into the rear, where they crouch behind the front seats. Once the car clears the area, they sit up straight. Ryan turns onto a side street, and Trace wriggles into the front passenger seat.

Trace gives Ryan a wink of approval as he checks out the jeep's interior. "She's a sweet one."

"I know. I wish she were mine."

"I wish we had a weapon."

"Who says we don't?"

"You're joking?"

Ryan grins. "Check the glove compartment. Do you know how to use a semi-automatic?"

"I go to the range regularly, but I've yet to buy my own."

"At least you're trained. Who knows what lies ahead of us? If you move things around, you'll also find pepper spray. We may need that as well."

"I see there's a reason you made Eagle Scout before me."

Proud, Ryan smiles. "Took it to heart—be prepared."

"And you've programmed the GPS already."

"Of course."

"Did you scan the jeep for trackers?"

"I rented it last night and assumed none. Why?"

"I keep seeing a white car behind us." Trace rubs his chin.

"No. It can't be." Ryan hits the steering wheel. "Look in the console. You should see my device."

"Got it." Trace turns on the scanner, and it lights up. The slow beeps become rapid when he moves toward the underside of the glove compartment. He finds the tracker and pulls it off.

"I can't believe it," Ryan mutters. "I'll pull over at that rest stop. Give me the tracker. You two duck down. It's good the windows are dark."

Ryan heads into the diner and purchases a cup of coffee to go. Minutes later, he leaves the store, drops his keys by another car, bends to pick them up, and puts the tracker on the other vehicle. All done, he gets back into the jeep. "When that driver takes off, so do we."

Lisa furrows her brow. "But they know our vehicle."

"Yeah, but we'll lose them once we hit serious traffic."

"Let's hope so. I can see them more clearly now. Looks like Elena and some guy."

"Describe him."

"Gray hair, weatherworn skin, beady eyes."

"Anything that distinguishes him from old men everywhere?"

"From here, not much."

Ryan says, "Look. The other car's backing out. I'll follow him until I see a way to lose the goons." He checks the GPS and points.

"See the tunnel up ahead? There's a side road that connects immediately after that. I'll make a sharp right, and we'll see if we lose them or not."

Ryan speeds ahead and positions for the turn. Abruptly, he comes around onto a gravel road. The jeep swerves erratically when he accelerates and climbs the hill, which abuts the side of the tunnel.

Wringing her hands, Lisa asks, "Anything?"

Trace shakes his head. "Not so far."

Ryan checks the rearview mirror and grips the wheel. "We'll follow this road to the next junction and decide what to do. On board?"

"I'm with you, buddy." Trace nods. "Since you had a tracker on this rental, it tells me you're a target like the two of us. We might have different tails following us, but the end game's the same."

"My thoughts exactly."

Ryan stops at the junction. "What's the vote? The mission still a go?" A few quick glances and he offers a thumbs up. "All right, partners, we're off to never-never land. How about some music?"

Trace finds a station they all like and sits back.

Forty-five minutes later, they arrive at Priscilla's Place, an unpaved dirt road in the woods.

"Good thing I rented a jeep. These potholes are canyons. And as you said, Lisa, there's no sign of civilization in this area. Trace, get the gun out just in case."

"What father would take his daughter here? Ridiculous."

Lisa shouts from the back seat, "I see it. There, on the left side. The log cabin."

Hardly detectable from the road, the lone hovel has knee-high weeds and untrimmed bushes. Barbed-wire fencing stretches around the property and tree limbs hang at the entrance threateningly.

"I'll pull in. Eh, on second thought, I'll back up close to the shack in case we need to race out of here. This looks a little too much like a late-night thriller."

Trace exits the jeep first and says to Lisa, "Over there on the right, is that the rock you saw?"

"I doubt it. I remember it being big."

"Yeah, and you were a tiny kid. It won't hurt to check it out. Come over and help me." Trace pushes the rock upward while Lisa searches underneath.

"I see a little metal pillbox. That must be it." She nabs it just before Trace lets the rock fall.

"I can't get the lid off."

Trace takes the box from her and jerks the lid open. Inside lies a strip of numbers. "This must be the combination number for a safe. Why else would he hide it?" He puts the paper strip into his pocket.

Ryan swats a mosquito on his arm and shoos a couple of annoying flies. "We're definitely in the woods."

Lisa approaches the front door and struggles to open the lock. "This can't be the key."

"Let me try." Trace takes the key, forces it in, and applies pressure to get the lock to turn. With multiple shoves, the door swings open.

A musty, unused-for-a-long-time stench hits them. Lisa stands at the doorway, taking it all in and trying to order her memories. Impatient, Trace and Ryan rush past her.

Lisa mutters, "What the heck, guys?"

"No time for daydreaming, Lisa," Trace snaps.

Reclaimed wood paneling stretches throughout the cabin. Maps of Europe, Russia, the Middle East, Southeast Asia, and the United States cover most of the paneling. In the center of the room, looking at the maps and the boxes on the floor, Trace says, "This is a war room. Dad must have plotted his trips here."

A memory hits Lisa. She watched her dad get upset or angry at someone or something when he stood exactly where Trace stands. And in a flash, she remembers why she felt afraid. She feared *him*. Lisa takes it all in and mumbles, "Rustic and secluded—perfect for your sordid activities."

Ryan studies a large calendar near the front door. It's heavily marked, and the last entry reads *July 8*. "Your dad must have come here a couple of months ago, or he marked that date for a future purpose."

Trace goes to his side to check it out. "Well, that's my birthday. Not that it ever meant much to him. And, like all the years before this, he didn't call or send a card. Your guess is as good as mine as to why he circled it."

"I won't even try to guess, my friend."

Lisa looks at the dates in the hope of remembering anything that might trigger a connection. Except for frustration, nothing arises, "I never paid much attention to his travels. But we should take the calendar with us. It might prove helpful down the road."

Trace notices Lisa's agitation and leans his shoulder to hers. "I know this is hard for you, but it will be over soon. We're getting closer by the day."

"It doesn't feel that way. Quicksand—miles of it. That's my experience." She turns and shuffles over to the fireplace. A half-burnt log rests in mounds of ashes.

Ryan says, "Stick with the plan, you two. In and out. We don't want to get caught here."

Trace makes a 360-degree turnaround. "Hey, I've counted thirteen boxes, and a quick look tells me they hold important documents and notes about travels. This may be the gold mine we've been searching for. Let's get as much as we can into the back of the jeep."

Lisa picks up one of the boxes and lugs it outside. As she lifts the rear door of the jeep, she hears an engine and runs back inside. "Someone's coming."

Trace and Ryan dash outside to the front of the cabin. Trace pushes Lisa behind him.

An old Ford pickup slows to a stop. Its once-white paint now shows patches of burnt-orange and steel-gray. A full-bearded driver with long, graying hair opens his window. "Hey, neighbor, I saw you drive in and wanted to make sure everything's okay."

Trace says, "Yeah, we're here to retrieve a few things for our father. He's been in an accident and needs his stuff to work on."

"I haven't seen him here for a while."

"He's traveled a lot recently."

"Your name? Curious is all. We don't get many visitors in this neck of the woods. Can't be too careful."

"I'm Trace Holmes." He reaches into his pocket, walks over to the man, and presents his driver's license. "You can take a look."

The stranger studies the card for a minute. "Okay. I live around the bend. If I can be of help, let me know."

"Will do. Thanks."

As he drives off, they all release a sigh.

Ryan says, "Let's move it. The next visitor may not be so friendly."

The trio hurries to load the back of the jeep.

Trace checks the time. "We need to get going."

Ryan shoves a final box into the jeep. "Copy that."

Lisa asks, "Trace, did you find a safe?"

Wide-eyed, he stares at Lisa. "I forgot all about it. I've got the strip of combination numbers in my pocket. There must be a safe somewhere. Did either of you notice loose floorboards?" Trace sees only blank stares. "Come on. Haven't you watched any cop shows lately? Let's make a fast check."

Back in the cabin, Lisa shouts, "Some loose boards here."

Trace and Ryan rush to her side and pull up a few planks. When they see a large Sentry safe, their mouths fall open.

"I'll try the combination." Trace takes the wadded paper from his pocket and enters the numbers. After a hefty tug, the door lifts open.

They freeze, momentarily. "What the … ?"

One-hundred-dollar bills fill the coffer, as well as bank account information and gold certificates. Trace reaches into the safe and brings out one of the stacks of bills. "I can't fathom how much money this is, but we can't take the safe with us. It must weigh several hundred pounds."

Lisa says, "I noticed some of the boxes aren't full. What if we empty a few and pack the money into those?"

Trace frowns. "Better than nothing. But then what? Where will we keep all this? We didn't expect to find money, and we're not prepared. This changes everything. Our suite isn't secure, and your home isn't either, Ryan. We can't go back now. So, what should we do?"

"Any place I can envision would put more people in danger," Ryan says.

Trace suggests, "We could turn it over to the police."

Lisa bites her bottom lip. "Yeah, but what if they're the problem?"

Trace sighs. "Better than us being the problem."

"Ditto that. There must be other options."

"Storage unit?" Ryan says. "Somewhere between here and New Rochelle?"

"Hmm. That's a neutral solution." Trace gives him a shoulder shove.

"I'll do a quick search. ... Found one. How about Ossining?"

"Ossining it is." Trace claps his hands. "Let's find boxes for the money and certificates and pack the jeep. We've got to get out of here ASAP. This must be a mob headquarters."

The three of them fill the boxes and replace the floorboards.

Trace asks Lisa, "You've got the calendar?"

"Yes."

"Okay, I'll lock the cabin. Let's hit the road."

After climbing into the jeep, Lisa fastens her seatbelt. "Now you know why I felt scared as a little kid. I knew something bad was going on. I still feel spooked. Just being here makes me feel like a criminal or someone evil."

"You're not a criminal, and you're not evil, but we're dealing with both," Ryan says. "Trace, keep the gun accessible. Lisa, you hold the pepper spray. On our return trip, we might encounter some ruffians."

Lisa takes the canister. "I've got it, and I'm ready."

"All right. Plug in the address."

Trace enters the address to George's Storage, and twenty-five minutes later, they pull into the complex.

Tucked away from the main street, and enclosed by a tall steel security fence, the storage units are barely visible from the road.

"Well, at least this is private," Trace says. He nods at Lisa. "Come with me to sign the rental papers."

They walk into the office and find an unshaven attendant seated behind the desk. The guy sets down his cell phone and looks at the siblings. "Monthly or yearly?"

"Monthly," Trace says.

Lisa scans the room and spots boxes and packing tape. "We'll have four boxes and this package of tape as well."

"We have more in the back room, ma'am. I'll show you." The man maneuvers his wheelchair to a side door and turns on the light. "There might be something in here that would help you."

Lisa notices his stumps and his dog tags. "Vietnam?"

"Yes, ma'am. U.S. Marine Corps. My last battle was the Tet Offensive in sixty-eight."

"My uncle served on a sub. He came back a changed man. Thank you for your service, Marine. You've given more than most of us ever will."

He studies her and sees her sincerity. "I'd do it again if I thought it would help our country. Some things are worth more than our lives."

"Wise words, sir, and timely. Thank you." Lisa selects a combination lock, a box cutter, and a pair of scissors, and returns to the front desk.

"Your unit is number seven-three-one—a five by ten-foot space. Go down the first row and make the second left. If you have any trouble, let me know."

"Will do."

Trace puts the items in the back seat with Lisa, as the cargo area is filled with the boxes from the cabin.

They approach the unit, and Ryan surveys the location of the cameras. "Keep your heads down, and let's unpack this jeep as fast as we can."

One-by-one, the group transfers the boxes into the unit. Lisa tapes the edges of the flaps to seal them. Partway through, she spots a stack of bank statements and holds them up. With tight lips, she shoves them into her briefcase. "I have a stack of documents I'm taking with us. They look important and might help us understand what's going on."

"Add this to it." Ryan hands Lisa a slip of paper. "It looks like a deed."

A few minutes later, Trace stands back and surveys the unit. "We're done, right? Let's get out of here." After Ryan and Lisa exit, he pulls down the rolling door and locks it.

Ryan checks the time. "Perfect—seven o'clock. We're on schedule. We'll reach the hotel within the hour. I'll drop you two off, return the jeep, and join you at the suite by late morning."

CHAPTER 11

Near the Westchester Tower Hotel, a red-tailed hawk soars above the treetops. Lisa watches it zoom in on an unsuspecting squirrel, dive swiftly, and capture the small creature with its talons.

"Daydreaming again?" Trace joins her on the deck, holding a steaming mug.

"I don't know. I guess I'm wondering if we're just prey—expendable feed for an unnamed monster. I've been watching that hawk. He waits for the right moment to attack. When he does, he doesn't miss." She shudders and hugs herself.

"Someone's watching us, Trace. We take all the precautions we can and try to outsmart this predator, but he finds us anyway. We have what he wants, even though we don't know what that is. Somehow, he needs us to get this unidentified item. That's the only reason we're alive." Lisa takes another sip of coffee and glances at her brother.

"You have a point, sobering though it is. I've looked at a few of the papers from the cabin, the ones you put in your briefcase. I found multiple bank accounts, which contain several hundred thousand dollars each. The monthly statements are concerning, and to top it off, the deposits come from unidentified international entities."

Lisa looks away and lifts her mug to her lips. "And whatever he was paid for, these assailants want."

"Maybe. What if he played them off each other?"

"Like a double agent?"

Trace nods and frowns. "Something like that. What if he was an informant, with the FBI and—or—Russia's FSB? If that were the case, it would be names, places, and key information they'd want."

"Dad had the perfect cover for an informant. And if you're right, it would explain the monthly deposits."

"Yep. He flew all over the world to meet with business leaders, but he could have met with military or political figures easily. Who would know? Makes you think about Elena, doesn't it?"

"I've always wondered about her."

"Yeah. Dad claimed she had no place to stay." Trace tosses his head back. "He and Elena would huddle into the early morning, whispering. Clearly, they knew each other well. Also, I remember Mom questioning Dad. Of course, she paid the price. No one could quiz him without repercussions."

"Maybe she knew. It's possible."

The doorbell rings. "It must be Ryan." Trace checks the peephole. "Hey, buddy. Long time no see. What can I get for you?"

"I could use some coffee with a bit of vodka."

"Seriously?"

"Rough morning."

"Yeah, seems like I know something about that. I'll doctor your coffee. Go on out to the deck. Lisa's looking forward to seeing you." Trace beams a mischievous smile.

Ryan returns a playful shove and walks out onto the deck, where he joins Lisa. "Hey, you look deep in thought. Something happen while I was gone?" He takes one of the empty chairs.

"Trace and I have considered various scenarios. Now we have more questions than answers, but we're playing with the notion that Dad operated as a double agent."

"Whoa, that's serious."

"It's the one thing that makes any sense in all this craziness."

Trace hands Ryan his coffee. "I've gone through the bank accounts. Regular deposits from unidentified international sources. These holdings are in addition to my parents' shared account."

Ryan's eyebrows lift. "This is serious stuff. What did you find, Lisa?"

"I'm not sure. Some of it's encrypted. There are several names and meeting locations, though."

"Could your dad have been a courier?"

"Is that different from a double agent?"

"I sure as hell don't know, but in my book, if you're just delivering messages from one place to another and not the one who acts on the instructions, it's less offensive. Dangerous but, somehow, more principled."

Trace crosses his arms and says, "Whatever he engaged in, I assume it was illegal. Why else would he have a private cabin in no-mans-land, stashes of cash, and all the rest?"

"Agreed. Illegal. That's why the FBI took the case."

"So, where do we go from here? We can't do this on our own." Trace looks at Lisa, waiting for her response.

A plane flies overhead and breaks the silence.

Trace continues to stare at Lisa and says, "I have the phone number for the FBI agent who tore up the house. Should I call him?"

"Do you trust him?"

"No, but who else do we trust? We have to do something. If we contact the police, the FBI will get involved anyway."

Ryan looks at Trace and back at Lisa. "So, what's the decision?"

Lisa diverts her gaze for a moment and stares at Trace. "Do you remember what we prayed for at Dad's grave?"

"Yeah, what of it?"

"I challenged him to redeem himself, and you followed with the demand, 'Show me there's something redeemable about your life.' What if he's doing that?"

"That's a big 'what if', and I'm not buying it. So, what's your point?"

"Let's wait another day before making our decision. When we go to the hospital, I'll talk with Dr. Schultz for a few minutes. He can help me gain some clarity."

Trace looks away and rubs the back of his head. "Seriously? We don't know whom to trust, and we've got stacks of illegal stuff in a storage container. Really, you want to wait?"

Lisa squirms. "Yes. I need to feel at peace about talking to the FBI, and I don't."

Trace throws his hands upward. "That's it for me. You win. I hope they don't kill us because we're postponing the inevitable. One more day, and no more."

"It's the right thing to do."

"Wish I could say the same. You trust signs and the unseen. I follow concrete, tangible evidence. But what the hell, I'm willing to take the risk for you, not because I believe we should."

"Understood. Thank you. When shall we leave for the hospital?"

Ryan glances back and forth at each of them. "After you fix me breakfast."

Lisa gives Trace her keys. "Could you drive? I'd like to sit in the back for this trip."

"Come here, sis." He throws his arms around her. "I don't agree with you about waiting, but I do love you."

Trace gets into the driver's seat and pulls out of the lot. He turns toward the freeway, and a squirrel darts across the street. He hits the brakes hard, which sends Ryan into the dashboard.

"Good grief, man, hanging out with you two is definitely a risky adventure."

And with that one comment, everyone relaxes a little and laughs. But a few minutes later, a tense silence returns.

Lisa bites her nails and stares out the side window. *What if Trace is right? What if they kill one of us? It would be my fault. What have I done? Maybe I should call it off.* At that moment, a raven swoops past and caws. She springs up in her seat. *A sign?*

They drive into the hospital parking lot, but before getting out, Trace says, "Did either of you notice the white sedan?"

"Yeah, I've been watching it through the side mirror," Ryan says. "Looks like Elena and the old guy. We need to keep extra alert. I suspect they're furious after this morning's stunt. Who knows where they ended up?"

Trace glances into the rearview mirror. "Three rows behind us. All right, let's do this. No wandering off by yourself, Lisa."

"Why are you focused on me? I'm not leaving your sight. Older brothers can be such a pain."

They climb out of the car and approach the hospital entrance. Once they've picked up their visitor passes, but before getting into the elevator, Lisa looks out to the parking area. Elena and her accomplice strut toward the lobby. Trace presses the elevator button for the second floor. It closes before the two mobsters reach them.

On the second floor, a police officer stands at each end of the hallway.

Lisa says, "While you guys visit Mom, I'll talk with Dr. Schultz and join you in a few minutes."

With a lift of their shoulders, Trace and Ryan offer tacit agreement.

Lisa walks down the hall to the psychologist's room. The patient sits by the window, finishing his breakfast.

"Hello, Dr. Schultz."

"Lisa. Come on in."

"Wow, a few short days and you look terrific."

"I feel great. It was only a surface wound, so I got lucky. How about a piece of toast?"

"I'll pass."

"How are you?"

"I won't lie. It's been difficult. I'd hoped we could have a brief session here. I need to make a big decision and don't trust myself."

"Because you don't trust the person or persons you're mulling over?"

"Correct."

"Police or FBI?"

"I don't know if I can trust either, but we have to do something."

"We? Your brother and you?"

"Yes, and a friend."

"When did you last see the FBI agents?"

"At our family home."

"Well, let's get started. There's another chair over by my bed. Pull it over."

Lisa fetches the chair and sets it near the window, at a side angle to Dr. Schultz.

"You know the process, so begin by taking a few deep breaths and move into a dream state."

Once Lisa grows quiet and settled, Schultz says, "Good. Now, float above the recent situation in your home. Go higher and higher until you can see the entire house. Tell me when you're there."

"I'm above the house now."

"From this heightened position, imagine the roof and the walls are transparent. Find the FBI Special Agent. Motion when you've done this."

Lisa signals with a hand movement.

"Move in closer to him and listen to what he says. Can you hear him?"

"Yes. He's on the phone. He's saying they haven't found it yet. 'There's got to be another hiding spot, sir. We've got a team tracking them, but so far, nothing. Nope, she's still in the hospital. She may never speak again. The daughter? I doubt she knows anything. She's sassy, though. The son? He's clueless and a pain to deal with. Will do. I'll have them tailed.'"

"Good. Now step away from the scene. Once you're in this room with me, let me know."

Slowly, Lisa opens her eyes and looks at the therapist.

"What did you learn?"

"He works for someone, and that person wants something specific."

"How did you feel? Did you trust him?"

"I felt danger, and no, I don't trust him."

"Let's do the same with the police captain. When did you see him last?"

"In the house. At the same time the FBI was there."

"Okay. Follow the identical process. Go into the dream state and rise above the house." Again, Schultz waits for her to relax. "Imagine the roof is transparent. Find the captain and tell me what he does."

Lisa sees the captain in the backyard. He smokes a cigarette and stares into the sky. One of the officers asks him about the floor.

"If there's no sign of prior disturbance, don't touch the floor."

"But the FBI operative ordered me to tear it up."

"What the hell for? I'll talk to him." Lisa watches as the captain speaks to the agent. The FBI guy insists on taking up the floor paneling. The captain scowls. "Then your men do it, not mine. I see no justification."

"The justification is because I said so."

"If you can live with that, then have at it, but I can't, and I won't have my men involved."

Dr. Schultz says, "This may be a good place to stop. When you're ready, drift back into the room."

Lisa squirms in her seat, and her foot taps against the floor.

"What did you discover?"

"The captain is trustworthy. He does things by the book. I sensed no personal agenda."

"So, of these two, you trust the police captain. Correct?"

"Yes."

"Now you have your answer. The only factor to consider is how much control the FBI has over the captain. If they suspect international involvement, the FBI will assert authority. That doesn't mean you can't talk with the police."

"But if I speak with the police, is what I say protected?"

"No. The police would be required to share whatever information they possess."

Lisa grows distressed, and Schultz says, "You have a gift. Sometimes, you know before others do. It's time to trust that gift. You'll find a way through this train wreck. Just keep close to your heart."

"Thank you. You don't know what this means to me."

"Of course, I do. I've been where you are now and faced comparable questions. It's not easy, but at least you have me. Next week, we'll meet in my office. The nurse told me she'll have my release papers ready today. We'll talk more then."

Lisa walks back to her mother's room and pauses at the doorway. Trace sits and tells stories, and their mom laughs. Ryan adds playful commentary and gesticulates while he talks. Lisa claps her hands and shouts, "Bravo," and they all laugh. "What a fun party. We need ice cream, don't you agree?"

"Let's order some right now." Trace uses the room phone and asks if they could have some ice cream. "There are four of us."

When he turns back to his mother, he smiles broadly. "The cafeteria will bring up ice cream."

Though she can only whisper her words, Katherine is radiant in the morning light and smiles and laughs freely. She motions for Lisa to come for a hug. With Lisa in her arms, she tells her to, please, visit Father O'Brien. "H-he has s-something for you."

"I look forward to meeting him. Saint Joan of Arc's Catholic Church?"

"Yes, d-dear."

A hospital orderly comes in with a tray, which holds four small bowls of ice cream. Trace reaches and takes one for his mom and one for him. "Time for a party." The orderly chuckles, sets down the tray, and departs.

Lisa watches while Trace feeds their mother and shares stories about his recent assignment in Tel Aviv. He talks about his bike tours along the Mediterranean and the local food. Their mom laughs at his antics and beams with joy while Lisa's heart swells with tenderness.

Ryan gives her a playful poke. "So, are you going to have some ice cream? We could toast with our spoons." His teasing smile makes Lisa laugh.

She takes her spoon and taps Ryan's. "What are we toasting?"

"Hmm, to laughter and friendship."

Their eyes lock and the smiles spread. "To laughter and friendship."

Lisa blushes soft pink.

CHAPTER 12

Excited as he walks out of the hospital, Trace shares what he saw. "Mom's getting better. When I told her about my last assignment, she was right there with me. She understood everything I said."

Lisa smiles. "Yes, and it warmed my heart immensely. She'll be okay. I know it."

"Well, what I saw—" Ryan says, "—was a family reunion. Can't beat that."

Trace puts his arm around Ryan's shoulder. "You're part of that family, buddy."

After climbing into the car, Trace does a double take when he looks in the rearview mirror. "We have company." He turns the ignition key and glances at Lisa and Ryan. "Shall we have some fun or try to lose them?"

Ryan checks the side mirror. "The white sedan?" Trace nods. "What kind of fun are you considering?"

Trace picks up his phone and punches in a number. "Captain Davis, this is Trace Holmes. You said I could call anytime. Well, I'm pulling out of the hospital parking lot, and there's this white sedan that keeps tailing us. It even tried to push us to the side of the road."

Ryan and Lisa focus on the conversation. When Trace hangs up, Lisa taps him on the shoulder. "What are you doing?"

"You'll see." Trace drives out of the lot, turns at the next intersection, and steers east. The white car follows. When he slows down, the sedan tries to bump them, as expected. At that, police sirens blare. Patrol cars surround the sedan, and officers step out of cruisers with guns pulled. Trace has led them to the New Rochelle Police Station.

Ryan bursts out laughing. "Brilliant! You always were the comedian."

Lisa rolls her eyes. "I confess I was worried."

"Now they're taken care of, where should we go?"

Lisa says, "Mom mentioned Father O'Brien. From what I recall, his church is a little north of here—Cortlandt, I think. We could talk with him and get lunch after."

"I'm good with that," Trace says. "But what does the priest have to do with anything?"

"I'm not sure, but Mom wants us to retrieve something from him."

"Of course, another mystery. Even when I was a toothless kid, I suspected our family was different from all my friends. What the hell—let's do it. You okay with the drive, Ryan?"

"Wouldn't miss this for the world. Besides, the police have the trackers in custody. Do you have a name for the church? I'll plug it into the GPS."

"Yeah, St. Joan of Arc."

"Got it. It looks like it's twenty minutes from here."

Driving through the downtown area of Cortlandt, Lisa notices several quaint stores she'd like to visit, while Ryan focuses on restaurants. He says, "I see several possibilities for lunch. Pizza, hamburgers, salads, … whatever's your pleasure."

Trace grins. "Good to know."

"Honestly," Lisa says. "Do you guys think about anything other than food? The world could end, and you'd want a hamburger."

"If the world was coming to an end, I'd order a steak." Ryan laughs. Then, after a glance at the GPS, he tells Trace to turn right at the stoplight.

After taking the turn, the church comes into view—an imposing 19th-century stone structure with tall steeples and beautiful stained-glass windows. The parking lot sits empty except for a few cars parked by the parish offices.

"You can tell this is a weekday," Trace says. "Lisa, you're Catholic, so you lead the way."

Lisa mock scowls. "You were raised Catholic just like me."

"That was a looong time ago, my dear, and it's been years since I've gone into a church."

"All right, it's not worth haggling over." Lisa climbs out of the car and follows a path, which leads to the Parish Center. Trace and Ryan trail behind. A sign with a list of church organizations hangs at the entrance to the one-story wooden structure and, beside it, a plaque with the pastor's name, Father Thomas O'Brien. She rings the doorbell.

"Can I help you?" an elderly woman asks.

"We'd like to speak with Father O'Brien. Is he available?"

"He's meeting with a parishioner right now, but he'll be free in a few minutes. Please, come in and have a seat in the foyer. May I ask who would like to see him?"

"Most certainly. My brother and I are here at our mother's request. Katherine Holmes."

The guys each find a chair while Lisa walks around the room. One of the walls has a list of benefactors engraved on brass plates. She looks through the names and spots Katherine Holmes. "I wonder if Mom attends Mass here rather than in New Rochelle. She's listed among the donors."

A tall, slender man with a balding crown enters the room just in time to hear Lisa's comment. "Yes, she attends Mass here regularly. I'm Father O'Brien, and I'm glad to meet you. Your mother speaks lovingly of you and your brother. How can I be of help?"

"Thank you, Father. I'm Lisa, and this is my brother Trace and our friend Ryan. Mom mentioned you today when we visited her at the hospital. She asked us to meet with you and said you had something for us."

"Hospital? I hope it's nothing serious."

"She's much better now, Father. But she's had a tough time recovering from a gunshot wound."

Father O'Brien's face contorts. "Oh my gosh, this is horrifying. Was anyone else hurt?"

"Yes. The shooter killed our dad. The police are working hard to bring the culprits to justice."

"I'm so sorry. My condolences to your family, and my sincere best wishes to your mother. I'll visit her this afternoon and take her Holy Communion. If you talk to her before I do, please let Katherine know I'm praying for her."

"I will. Thank you."

"She reminded me several times that you'd visit someday, but I never imagined these circumstances." He shakes his head in disbelief and touches the cross hanging from his neck. "Please, follow me."

Slowly, he walks outside to a flower garden, where a vast spread of daisies covers the perimeter abutting the stone fence. "Several times a year, your mother visits. She weeds, trims, and sometimes cuts the daisies to take home with her. She keeps her tools in the shed to the left."

While strolling through the flowers, Lisa notices a memorial sign and stops. It reads *Robbie's Garden, My Beloved Angel.* She takes Trace's hand and points to the sign.

The priest sees their interest. "Katherine likes to say that her baby Robbie is playing happily in Heaven. She buried a remembrance box next to the sign. That's what she wants you to have now." He turns to Trace, "There's a trowel in the shed if you'd like to dig it up."

Trace tilts his head to the side and considers the priest's offer. For a moment he hesitates then fetches the garden tool. After a quick glance at Lisa, he digs. A few strong thrusts later, he hits something hard—a steel box inside a sealed plastic container. Trace pulls it out, brushes off the dirt, and gives it to his sister.

Lisa unseals the mystery container and peeks inside. Her face drops. "It's filled with documents and other papers."

The priest nods, "If you'd like to go through the box in our reading room, you're welcome to do so. It's private, and you can close the doors."

"Thank you, Father. We'd appreciate that."

Father O'Brien takes them through a side door of the Parish Center to the room. "Your mother likes to sit in here and read. The upholstered chair by the window is her favorite spot. She claims Robbie joins her. I don't know about that, but she always leaves smiling."

Lisa glances about the space. A picture hangs between two built-in bookcases. She walks over and raises her hand to her mouth. The photo shows Robbie as a toddler chasing a butterfly among the daisies. With an incredulous expression, she turns to the priest.

His face glows. "Your mother funded and decorated this room. Lovely, don't you think? Take all the time you need. I'll leave you alone now." He walks out and closes the door.

Trace joins his sister and wraps his arm around her shoulders. "I remember Robbie's giggles and fascination with butterflies, but I've never seen this picture until now."

Ryan joins the siblings. "I can imagine Robbie visiting your mom here." He darts a peek at Lisa. "I suspect her other-worldly trait runs in the family."

Trace gives him a playful shove. "Let's get to work." They cross to a round table in the center of the room and take a seat.

Lisa frowns. "I'm almost afraid of what we'll discover."

"We don't have a choice," Trace says. "Mom wants us to have this for a reason. Hopefully, whatever's inside will help us with our situation." He empties the items onto the table. "If we each share the burden, it shouldn't take us long. As we finish reading the documents, let's stack them back into the box so we can keep some order."

Trace distributes the papers and comes across a message from their mother.

"Hey, here's a letter from Mom. I'll read it out.

> *'Dear kids, if you are reading this, it's because I am incapacitated, or I've joined Robbie in Heaven. You might wonder why I didn't act on the information in this box. Well, I chose to stay silent to protect you both. You mean everything to me. You are wise. Use this information carefully. I love you with all my heart, Mother.'"*

"Whoa, that's heavy," Ryan says. "It's like a prisoner wrote it."

"Probably an accurate assessment," Trace says. "Let's see what's here." Trace picks up the top sheet. "This is interesting. It's Dad's Four-F military classification. It states he was unsuitable for military service because of behavioral disorders. Interesting. He always told us his eyesight kept him out of the service." Trace shakes his head and shoves the document back into the box.

Lisa takes a paper. "I have Robbie's death certificate." Her eyes widen, and her eyebrows raise as she reads. She looks at Trace. "It lists the reason for death as blunt force trauma to the brain. A fractured skull."

She takes a deep breath. "I presumed this to be the case but seeing the death certificate is heart-wrenching. Dad claimed he fell down the stairs. This proves otherwise. He murdered Robbie, intentionally or accidentally." Lisa cups her head in her hands.

Ryan picks up a birth certificate. He studies it and says nothing.

"What do you have?" Trace asks.

"I'm not sure, but I think you should take this." He hands it over to Trace. "From first glance, it looks like your birth certificate."

Trace reaches for it. "I wondered where it was." The color drains from his face when he reads the document. He pushes back in his chair.

Ryan hands him a newspaper clipping. "I believe this goes with the certificate."

Trace reads it and looks away, and—rubbing his head—he exhales slowly. "I didn't expect this."

"What's going on?" Lisa leans forward.

Trace's voice cracks when he answers. "Dad wasn't my biological father. My birth father died in a car accident when I was two. Jose Rivera—a landscaper. I was his only child." He looks down. "I-I don't know what to say."

Lisa reaches for the document and scrutinizes the content. "When Mom gets better, you can talk with her about all of this. She's a free person now, Trace. She can explain."

"But why keep it a secret all these years?"

"Remember the threats Dad made to her? He would kidnap us if she ever spoke about anything. Dad wanted total control of her life, and that meant cutting ties with people to whom she might—consciously or unconsciously—divulge information. Mom was trapped."

"I get that. He was super paranoid and even taunted her about minor things. At least now we're beginning to understand why."

"Do you recall asking her about our ancestry? About why your skin was darker than mine?"

"Yeah. She said we had some ancestors who came from Spain. After she said that, I didn't think any more about it."

"She gave you a clue, though. I suspect that was the most she could do."

"Probably. Who knows what Dad would have done?"

Ryan hands Trace a ring, which holds a single pearl. "This was in the envelope with a note attached."

Lisa and Trace read the short note. In scratchy handwriting it says,

To my precious Katherine, with all my heart, Jose.

Trace covers his face with his hands. "I don't know why I feel emotional. I didn't know this man Jose. But I wish I did. Mom loved him." His shoulders fall. "I'll talk with her when the timing feels right."

Lisa looks at Ryan, and a tear runs down her cheek. They wait until Trace composes himself.

"Is there anything else?" Ryan asks.

Lisa presents three photos. The images show their father meeting separately with Elena, Joe Gagnon, and the department store tycoon.

"You've got to be kidding me. And we thought Mom didn't know anything."

Lisa bites her bottom lip. "I can't help but wonder how she got these pictures."

"Your mother is a sharp woman," Ryan says. "I suspect she hired an investigator."

"That doesn't seem like her."

"No? Look at this stack of airline ticket receipts. During this one trip, your dad flew to Paris, then to Kyiv, then to Phnom Penh, and—finally—home."

"When was that?"

"Looks like four months ago. He stayed in Paris for three days, Kyiv for a week, and spent the rest of the time in Cambodia. A little odd, don't you think?"

Trace says, "To say the least." He leans in to read for himself. "But everything about him was odd. It would be normal for him to take off to some meeting and stay gone a month. For me, it was a relief. No yelling, no threats, no beatings. I was glad when he'd leave."

"Lisa, what about you?"

"I don't know what I thought. It was his job, and I never asked questions. He treated me differently than Trace. Now we know why."

"What would your mom say?"

"She didn't say anything one way or another. She'd tell us that he was going to a meeting here or there. We never knew when he'd return. We learned to live with the mystery."

"So why did your mom save these flight receipts for you? What did she want you to understand?" Both Trace and Lisa focus on Ryan, who tilts his head and flings his hands in the air. "Why would she have kept these receipts for you?"

Trace looks at them both intently. "She wants us to understand that Dad wasn't who we thought he was. He had multiple lives, and we intersected briefly with him a few days each month."

"Did you ever wonder why this trip, or any trip, took a month?"

"Never."

"What about you, Lisa? Did you ever wonder?"

"No. I was younger and tried to stay out of his way."

"Well, as a guest at this party, this is what I see. Your dad used the excuse of an international meeting to take care of business unrelated to his job. He was engaged in something undercover, either with our government or some clandestine entity."

Lisa's eyes widen. "What are you suggesting?"

"Just stating the obvious. I'm not suggesting anything."

An uncomfortable silence fills the room.

Trace breaks the tension and asks Lisa, "When Gagnon shot Dad, what were his exact words before he killed him?"

"'*Where is it?*' And then, after Dad said he didn't have it, Gagnon said, '*Your choice,*' and shot him."

Trace taps his fingers. "So, he'd agreed to provide something. They must have paid him in advance. Then he claimed he didn't have whatever it was. Do you suppose the thing might be in the storage unit?"

Ryan shrugs. "It's worth a look."

Lisa shudders. "You're right, but I hate the thought of going through that stuff."

"Me too," Trace says. "But we need to figure out the 'what' before we call the police. The intruders demolished the house for a reason. There's either an object of international importance or something incriminating about some immensely powerful people. Maybe both."

Ryan runs a hand over the stacked papers. "Yep, you read my mind. A list is easy to hide. A precious jewel as well. I'll tag along to wherever you two want to go, but this outsider votes for a trip to the storage unit."

"All right, let's go say goodbye to Father O'Brien." Trace holds the metal box and carries it to the priest's office.

Lisa says, "Father, we're ready to leave now. Might we take this box with us? There's personal information in it."

"Of course. Your mother meant this for you and Trace. Not me." The priest stands and walks out with them. "I've known your mother for many years. She's a beautiful woman inside and out, and you were absolutely her priority. I suspect you're questioning things about your father's business affairs. Just let me say, our loving God measures each of us by the love we offer others. Such measurement has no timeline. Your father may be learning to love now, in ways he wasn't capable of while alive. Redemption isn't magic. It's not a one-time event. Rather, redemption is a process of letting go into *Love* itself. I pray your father has discovered that one *Love* and is learning to extend it to his family."

CHAPTER 13

Trace pulls out of the church parking lot with tires screeching. In the back seat, Lisa stares out the side window. No one speaks. After a sharp turn onto Route 9, Ryan loses his balance and grabs the armrest. "How about I drive?"

Trace's jaw tightens. "I'm fine."

"Okay, just offering. I've got the directions to the storage unit, and according to the GPS, it's less than ten minutes from here. Do we eat now or later?" When neither Trace nor Lisa reply, he says, "I'll take that as *later*."

A lot of heavy silence, and a few minutes later, finds the trio rummaging through the boxes.

"I can barely breathe in here." Lisa wipes her forehead. "The temperature must be over a hundred-and-twenty degrees."

Even with the door of the storage unit wide open, no air circulates in the metal container. Lisa, Trace, and Ryan work quickly and flip through stacks of paper, but not fast enough. Sweat rolls down their reddened cheeks.

"This is hell." Trace pants. "Let's take what we need and get out of here."

"Some of this isn't in English," Ryan says. "Did your dad know another language?"

Trace rubs sweat from his eyes. "Not that I'm aware of, but he could have used a translator."

"Here's something strange." Lisa holds out a spreadsheet. "It looks like payments for different assignments."

Trace takes it and studies the list. "We're taking this one with us." He finds a manila envelope, which contains photos of Federal officials with Gagnon, Elena, and their dad. "This one may be worth killing over. We'll take this as well."

Ryan holds up a sheet. "This might be the evidence we're looking for. It's a handwritten assignment. '*Pick up the package at the usual meeting place in Kyiv. Deliver it to agent Pham.*' From what I see, your dad was transporting valuable information or items. And these folks didn't trust normal channels of communication."

Trace grows impatient. "Anything else, guys? We need to get out of here before we're detected or before we die of heat exhaustion. I've sweated through my shirt."

"As have I. Let's hit the road," Lisa says.

Ryan nods. "There's a convenience store on the corner. Let's stop there and get some water."

A couple of minutes later, they park, and Ryan hops out of the car. "I'll get the water. Keep the air conditioning running."

Lisa pokes Trace's shoulder. "Could we take a detour to the house before we go back to the hotel?"

"We could, but why? What are you looking for?"

"Don't know. We're missing something, though. Let's circle through it one more time."

"Fine. We'll drive there first, then back to the hotel."

Ryan returns. "Water, anyone?"

"Thanks." Trace takes a bottle and pulls out of the parking lot. Once on the road, he relays the change in plans to Ryan.

"I'm here for the ride. You two lead the way."

Between gulps of water, Ryan says, "It seems we have confirmation your dad was a courier. What are your thoughts?"

Trace tightens his lips. "When you first suggested that idea, I discounted it. But not now."

Ryan looks at him. "You remember something?"

"An experience keeps bugging me. I was a student at Boston University, and I took the Amtrak to Penn Station to come home. One time, I had a late train. It arrived at half past ten at night. To my amazement, Dad picked me up. But there was a catch. He told me he needed to speak with a friend at a bar on Fifty-Seventh Street. We went there, and Dad disappeared. I waited in the car, but after a while, I decided to go in and have a beer. I ordered and watched him. I couldn't see the face of the person he spoke to, but I saw Dad give the man a large envelope, and after that, the mystery man gave him a small but thick envelope. Dad shoved it into his jacket pocket, and they stood and shook hands like two businessmen. The mystery person left via the back of the bar, and he never turned around."

"And you think this transaction is an example of exchanging information for payment?"

"Yeah. At the time, I thought it peculiar, but in my family, we lived with the peculiar. I asked Dad what it was about, and he snapped at me. Told me it was none of my business. Then he switched it on me and wanted to know if I'd improved my physics grade. I told him I was working hard. You know what he said? He told me, 'I paid my friend Bob to take my final exam at one of Purdue's regional campuses. Nobody knew me there. Bob signed in, claimed he was me, and aced the test. I ended up with an A in the course. There's a way around every problem. Find it.'"

Lisa gasps. "So, what did you do?"

"Frankly, I decided to screw him. I aced the exam on my terms. I got a tutor and studied like hell. It was my way to show Dad I was better than him."

Lisa wipes teary eyes and struggles to say something. "You were always better than him."

Five minutes later, Trace drives onto their cul-de-sac and parks near the house on the street. A police car, a painter's van, and a pickup crowd the driveway.

Lisa takes a long swallow of water. "I hate to say this, especially given our earlier conversation, but we need to try to think like Dad. If he were hiding something, where would he put it? He liked to play with clues. You'd never get a straight answer out of him. So, if we're to make progress, we need to consider clues."

Trace opens his door. "You're probably right, though thinking like him makes me nauseous."

They walk toward the house and greet the officers sitting outside in their patrol car.

"All going well, sir?" Trace asks.

"It's been a quiet day, except for the workmen's radio. We've asked them to turn it down a couple of times. Somehow, it climbs back up."

"Sorry about that, officers. I'll speak with them."

Inside the house, Lisa calls, "*Hello*?"

A guy turns, gives them a *whatever* look, and returns to his work. The other workers don't respond.

Lisa surveys the destruction. "It looks like things are pretty much where they were when we last visited. What a nightmare." She steps over a shattered Japanese jug and notices the gutted grandfather clock. In their parents' bedroom, her mom's jewelry box lies open on the bed, its costume jewelry spread across the bare padding. Lisa fingers a beaded necklace she'd made for her mom at summer camp. Then, wiping her eyes, she turns and circles back to the living room.

The stuffing from the couch blankets the floor. Lisa picks up a piece. "Strange—they not only pulled out the stuffing, but they also shredded it. Whatever they're looking for is small."

Ryan snatches a chunk and examines it. "Good observation."

"What did you say? I can't hear through all this racket?"

"I can fix that." Ryan walks over to the radio and turns it down. Soon, four pairs of annoyed eyes stare at him.

"Don't touch our stuff," a painter says.

"Hey, we're only here for five minutes, but we can't hear one another. Give us a few moments of peace."

The painters exchange glances and return to their work. Ryan repeats what he said to Lisa.

Trace goes from room to room to check on the progress. He returns with a thumbs up. "They've repaired the walls. Taped, spackled, and sanded. One more day, and I believe they'll finish the painting."

Lisa asks, "You took photos, right?"

Trace salutes. "Yes, ma'am."

Lisa nods. "I'll take a few more. The answer is here. I feel it." She walks over to the pile of wall hangings. One-by-one, she picks them up and pauses. "Trace, come here. Have you seen this one before?"

Trace joins her and looks at the painting. "No. Never."

"Dad would leave a clue—nothing obvious but something that would make us pause and consider possibilities. Do you think this could be a clue?"

Trace mumbles, "Two kids on the beach ... wait a minute. This is the cottage he rented for the summer in Old Lyme, CT."

Lisa studies the dwellings along the water. "You're right. I remember that blue house in the distance. Mom thought it beautiful." She turns the painting over, and in small print, it reads, *Old Lyme, CT*. "Oh my gosh, he's leading us to our summer cottage."

Ryan rests two fingers against his chin. "It's a wild guess, but are we taking a trip there tomorrow?"

"You read my mind. I'll check to see if the rental is vacant. We're past the summer vacation crowd. Schools are in session, and people are at work. Who knows, we might get lucky. I'll give the agency a call." Trace escapes into the kitchen where it's quieter. He signals a thumbs up to Lisa and Ryan. "I'd like to rent a cottage for a couple of nights. How about tomorrow? Okay, okay. If you send the parking pass to my email, I'll print it and bring it with me. My credit card? Yes. Here goes."

While her brother sorts out the rental, Lisa turns to Ryan. "Should I bring this painting with us?"

"Might prove helpful. But if you do, keep it locked in the car. I don't trust the security at the hotel."

"Agreed. I'd considered just that."

Trace walks back into the room and looks triumphant. "We have the cottage for the next couple of nights. We don't need to stay there, but this gives us the freedom to do what we want. Let's be extra careful not to attract the attention of Elena and her sidekicks. I don't want that cargo on this trip."

"I almost forgot. Give me a minute." Lisa darts back to her parents' bedroom and searches through the bathroom drawers for her mother's hairbrush. Once she finds it, she scurries out the front door. At the driver's side of the car, she jerks away when a passing delivery truck swerves and nearly hits her.

"Watch out." Ryan yanks her out of harm's way.

Lisa tries to catch her breath. "If you hadn't been here, I might have gotten hit."

Ryan holds her a few seconds longer than needed.

Trace breaks up the two. "Hey, let's move it." To his sister, he says, "Why do you have that brush?"

"When it's time to go home, I'd like to fix Mom's hair, and this is the brush she uses."

"Good thinking." Behind the steering wheel, Trace pulls away from the curb and turns in the direction of the hotel. "As frustrating as this day has been, we've made some progress. There are indications Dad was a courier. We believe the mystery item is small. And we're guessing the beach rental is a clue. When we get to the hotel, we can go through some of the things in the trunk. We might find other pointers."

Ryan glances at Trace. "Have there been any international heists?"

"None that I know of, but something major's going on. Look at the four people involved—Joe Gagnon, a felon and hitman; Elena, a spy and—possibly—a hitman as well; an old scary mystery guy; the billionaire owner of a department store. Quite the foursome."

"And we're in the middle of it," Ryan says. "The FBI followed your father for some time, or they used him."

"The more I learn, the more I think they did both." Trace grips the wheel and eases into the hotel parking lot. "Let's empty out the trunk. With the three of us, we might only need to make one trip."

Once in the suite, Trace motions for Lisa and Ryan to put the boxes and papers in the hallway closet.

Lisa looks out the windows. "Let's sit outside. There's a nice breeze, and we all could use some fresh air."

Ryan stretches his legs and suggests they consider dinner. "We could even go downstairs to the restaurant. I don't know about you guys, but since we're not going to solve this puzzle tonight, I need food and drinks. Dieting by starvation isn't my thing."

Lisa laughs. "I'm with you but let's order in. Trace and I will leave for the hospital soon and eating in will help save time."

"The company's good and drinks are on the house. I can't complain."

"You crack me up. Give me your order, and I'll call for food service. We can relax out here, eat, and have a few drinks. Sound good?"

Ryan chuckles. "How about a medium rare steak?"

"Would you accept a hamburger substitute?"

"Why not? With plenty of fries."

"Make that two orders," Trace says.

Lisa fetches the room service menu from the kitchen and makes the call. Finished, she pours herself a glass of wine and strolls outside.

"Wait a minute," Trace says. "One of us should go light since we're driving to the hospital later."

"Aren't you driving?" Lisa frowns at her full glass.

Trace offers, "I could."

"Hmm, in that case, I think Mom won't mind if I have a drink or two."

CHAPTER 14

The wind tosses leaves and pieces of paper across the street and onto the windshield. Trace swerves to miss a rolling cardboard box while Lisa holds onto the door grab handle.

"Where did this come from? It was a sunny day, last I checked." Her brows furrow as she stares at the dark clouds. "Was the forecast for rain?"

"Yeah, a squall line's coming through but, hopefully, it won't hit until we're back at the hotel." Trace makes a sharp turn. "Did you bring an umbrella?"

"Nope. Mine's at my apartment upstate. I didn't pack one for the trip. I thought I'd be gone just for the weekend."

"I didn't bring one either," Trace says. "Even if we get wet, it won't matter to Mom."

Lisa studies her brother. "Will you ask her about your birth certificate?"

"I'm not sure. It depends upon how she feels."

"She wouldn't have mentioned Father O'Brien if she didn't want you to see it."

"I know."

"Doesn't it feel like we're characters in some late-night slasher? Can't trust anybody, and nothing is as it seems."

"I get it, and yes, this whole experience is surreal." Trace stares straight ahead, eyes narrowed, and lips tightly closed.

"Are you okay?"

"Yes and no. I have a lot of lingering questions, and some of those questions affect me personally. My life, at least how I've understood it, is pretty much up in the air. That's a lot to swallow."

"You're not alone."

"I know, but it's a solitary trip. You can't walk it for me. At best, we can travel that path together."

He pulls into the hospital parking lot and hits the brakes.

Trace turns to Lisa and exhales through puffed lips. "Ready?"

Before they reach the revolving doors, Lisa stretches for his hand. "Together, Trace."

"Together it is."

Neither speaks as they head to the second floor. The elevator chimes their arrival and the doors open. Nurses wave hello, and unknown visitors push past them into the elevator.

"People can be so rude. At least they could say, 'excuse me.' That old guy bumped right into me. Did you see that?" Lisa scowls.

"I wasn't paying attention. Who knows, maybe the dude's wife is on this floor," Trace says.

"True. Still ..."

When they near their mother's door, they hear a familiar voice.

"I'll see you tomorrow, Katherine." Father O'Brien turns and meets Trace and Lisa at the doorway. "What a wonderful surprise. It's good to see you two again. I had a great visit with your mother. I'll come back tomorrow, so maybe we'll see each other again. God bless you." And with that, he disappears down the hall.

Trace and Lisa move to their mother's side.

"He's s-so kind," Katherine whispers. "He b-brought Holy Communion."

Lisa takes her mom's hand. "When we met him at Saint Joan of Arc's, he told us he'd visit and bring you the sacrament. I'm glad we got to see him again. How do you feel?"

"Much b-better." Katherine reaches out her hand toward Trace. "How are you, son?"

He lowers his head and meets her eyes. "Good. I have questions about my birth father." Trace watches his mom. "Someday we can talk about that, but not right now. You need to rest."

Their mother squeezes his hand. "You have a f-family. A large family." Lovingly, she looks into Trace's eyes.

"Rivera family?"

"Yes. T-there are m-many of them." She smiles.

Trace glances downward and back to their mother. "Why wasn't I told about them?"

"Y-your father wouldn't allow me to say anything. I f-feared what he m-might do. The Riveras understood and w-were protective of you."

"At the right time, I look forward to hearing more and meeting all of them."

"S-soon, son, soon."

She motions for him to draw near, and in a barely audible voice, she says, "F-fishers Island. Father K-kerry."

A nurse makes her rounds and stops to check Katherine's vitals. To Trace and Lisa, she says, "Your mother needs to rest."

"Thank you, nurse. We'll leave now." Trace bends and whispers. "We'll go see the priest tomorrow." After a final hug, Lisa and her brother say goodbye.

In the hallway, Lisa asks, "What did Mom mumble to you? Could you understand her?"

"She mentioned Fishers Island and Father Kerry. It must be important because she whispered it. I told her we'd go there tomorrow."

Lisa rubs her lower lip. "Odd. I don't remember ever going to that island."

They make their way toward the exit and walk past the waiting room. Lisa jolts and stops. The same old guy who bumped into her at the elevator sits in the waiting area. All at once, Lisa remembers seeing him at the funeral and realizes he's been following them. There's no mistaking his identity.

Lisa tugs on Trace's hand. "That's the guy who accompanies Elena."

"You're right. I'll get Security."

Lisa keeps her focus on the man and notices his tattoo, half visible under his short-sleeved shirt. It shows the symbol of an army medic.

The man realizes his cover is blown and gets up to leave. Lisa dashes in front of him. "Why are you following me? Threatening my family? Who are you?"

The man pushes her aside, but she shoves back in front of him. "Your tattoo tells me you were an Army Combat Medic. What happened to the oath you took?"

Security arrives. "Sir, we need to ask a few questions."

"Back off." The guy pulls a semi-automatic from his pocket. A woman screams and runs. "Sit down," the gunman yells.

The front desk staff calls 911. Within minutes, multiple sirens wail.

The guy's nostrils flare, and he scowls at the staff and visitors. With the weapon in front of him, he sweeps the muzzle across the room, ready to fire, and backs out of the entrance doors.

Those in the waiting room area scramble to the windows to watch the police confront the former medic.

"Put down the weapon," an officer with a bullhorn shouts. "We've got you surrounded. Hospital security guards are behind you. There is no place for you to run."

Another siren blares, and Captain Davis arrives on the scene.

When the captain walks to the front line, the gunman yells, "I'd rather die than spend my life in jail." He raises his gun and aims at the captain. The police respond with full force, multiple shots sound, and the man falls to the ground, motionless.

The captain approaches the nearest police officer. "What the hell is this about, officer?"

"The gunman pulled a semi-automatic inside the hospital. He threatened visitors, and the front desk called us. When he came outside, we were waiting. We're checking his ID now."

"Let me know as soon as you get the info. I'm going inside." The captain steps through the entrance doors and spots Trace and Lisa.

"This wouldn't involve you two, would it?"

Lisa dips her head. "Maybe, sir."

The captain gives a sour grin. "Why am I not surprised?"

Soon, reporters crowd the waiting area and clamor to speak with the chief. About a foot taller than most, his presence commands. At a calm pace, accentuating each word, he says, "I will speak with you when I have something to say. We should have information soon. Please, let me do my work now. I arrived last on the scene and need to catch up."

The captain turns to Lisa and Trace. "You two sure keep my men busy. Let's find a room where we can talk." He signals to a person at the front desk and leads the way to a private sitting room.

He takes a chair and studies them. "How's your mom doing?"

Trace says, "She's better. The progress is slow, but she understands and can speak now, and the doctor told us she'll walk again."

"Good to hear, good to hear. So, how are you two?" He puts his finger on his chin and observes the pair.

Lisa says, "It's not been easy, Captain, but now Trace is here, I feel much better."

"I've taken a month's leave from work to help with this mess. I can extend that time if necessary."

The captain leans forward and scratches the back of his neck. "Have you figured out what's going on yet?"

"Not exactly, but we know Dad was involved with something dangerous, something international, and probably illegal."

The captain nods a few times and checks his cell. "Looks like we have some information on the old army medic. Alexander Roberts. Served in Desert Storm, and like thousands of other soldiers, he suffered chemical intoxication—The Gulf War Syndrome. Also, had terminal brain cancer, which he blamed on his service in the Middle East."

In dismay, Lisa covers her mouth. "That's why he got involved with Elena. Anger against his country. Now I feel awful for calling him out."

"Interesting." The captain puckers his lips. "You feel bad for a criminal, who would have killed me if my men hadn't responded first. He had a loaded gun and would have used it."

"When you put it that way, no."

"What other way is there?"

Lisa stumbles for words. "I-I guess I feel sad he had cancer."

The captain pushes back in his chair. "Everyone in this place is either dying or close to it. Life doesn't play favorites. This guy got the raw end, and the military shares some responsibility for that. But his actions? Those are his alone. No one else's." The captain looks at each of them. "I've seen a lot in my days. This guy wanted to die on his terms. He had no reason to live and didn't care if you did either. He felt angry at life and was dangerous because of that."

Trace says, "Captain, the people who follow us, what are they looking for?"

"I have no idea, but they'll stop at nothing to get it." He studies Trace. "Off the record, do you carry?"

"No, sir."

"Do you know how to use a weapon?"

"Yes. I go to a gun range often."

"You need to consider options." He taps his fingers on the table. "It'll escalate now."

CHAPTER 15

Lisa and Trace arrive at their suite just as the crescent moon disappears behind clouds and the pitch-black sky comes alive with lightning strikes. Booms of thunder warn of approaching rain. Within minutes, sheets of water pound the deck in a deafening roar. The siblings stand and watch the display through the picture windows.

"Someone's been here," Lisa whispers to Trace.

"You're sure?"

"Positive. I left my briefcase on the couch with its shoulder strap draped across the arm. Look where it's at now."

Trace turns and stares. "Could Ryan have picked it up?"

"I was the last one out of the suite this afternoon."

Trace squeezes her hand. "Check to see if anything's missing."

"I will. But, going forward, it'll be wise to keep important papers in the car trunk."

"Probably best. I'll text Ryan about tomorrow." Trace taps on his cell phone, and Lisa reads from his side.

> *Change in plans. Can you stop over, or can we meet you at your place?*

The response is immediate.

> *I'm nearby. See you in fifteen.*

"The rain's stopped. That was a fast squall. Let's wipe down the deck chairs and sit outside." Lisa fetches a stack of towels and throws one at Trace.

"Now you're getting bossy." He chuckles and gets to work.

Lisa finishes drying the last chair and smiles at her brother. "That wasn't so hard, now was it?" She circles back into the kitchen, pours herself a glass of wine, and prepares a tray of cheese and crackers. Back out on the deck, she positions her chair to better see the stars.

Trace grabs a beer and joins her. Lisa takes a sip of wine and leans back to look at the sky. "Extraordinary."

"Yep, I always thought so."

Lisa swirls her wine and says, "Do you know why Mom mentioned Father Kerry?"

Trace gulps his beer and bends forward. "Maybe when we go to the cottage, we can figure it out. Fishers Island isn't far—just a short ferry ride from New London. Dad loved the place. I remember going there a few times."

"Strange. I don't remember it at all."

"You will. I guarantee it. That's where you found Priscilla."

"Found?"

Trace grins and teases with a wink. "Got your attention, didn't I? Yep, there was a little boutique with dolls and other girly things on the main street. You ran inside before Mom could stop you and got a doll. You wrapped your arms around it and refused to let it go. Dad said, 'Ah, I bet you'd like to name her Priscilla.' You jumped up and down and shouted *yes*, and that was that. You had a new doll."

"Hmm. He named her after the street that leads to the cabin. Brilliant, just brilliant. I should have expected as much."

"Right. And you fell for his scheme." Trace laughs, but the mirth holds bitterness.

"I was a kid, for cripes sake."

A rapping noise sounds at the door. Trace stands and strides through the suite to welcome Ryan, who says, "Hey, long time no see. I thought you might have an extra beer, maybe some nibbles."

"We have both. Go on out to the deck, and I'll join you there."

Lisa looks up. "You've missed a lot of excitement, my friend."

"I see a pattern and it's a simple one. Trouble follows the Holmes clan."

"I hate to admit it, but I see the same pattern, and it's unnerving. Did Trace tell you what happened at the hospital?"

"Not yet."

"We were walking past the waiting room and spotted the old guy who travels with Elena. He saw us and pulled a gun. The staff called the police. He went outside and pointed his gun at the captain, and the police shot him."

Ryan stares at Lisa, and a slow smile spreads across his face while he shakes his head. His cheeks blanch. "I'm sure it was scary, but I've seen this movie before."

"You don't believe me?"

"Of course I do. Who could make this up?"

Trace passes Ryan a beer. "Sharing war stories?"

"Nah, just catching up with your day. I'm sorry I missed the fireworks."

"I bet." Trace eases into his chair. "We have another destination tomorrow. Mom mentioned Fishers Island and Father Kerry. She didn't explain but acted as though the two are of critical importance. That's why I texted."

"You want to go tomorrow?"

"We'll be in the area already. The ferry's a short drive from the cottage, but we'll need to take extra precautions. After today's altercation, we're in the crosshairs."

"Have you worked out a plan?"

"Only a rudimentary one. Lisa and I will take a cab to Five Islands Park and stop in front of the restaurant. You'll have a rented car and will wait for us in the back of the restaurant. I'll help pilot us to Old Lyme, where we'll check out the cottage. After that, we'll board the ferry in New London and cross to Fishers Island. How does that sound so far?"

"Works for me. And meeting at the back of the restaurant might confuse Elena."

"Yeah. The captain warned us the stakes are extremely high. Even asked if I knew how to use a weapon."

Playfully, Ryan throws his head back and raises his brows. "This is getting interesting. What time? Early, right?"

"How's seven o'clock?"

"No problem."

"Another beer?"

"I'm good. I need to get a rental and ready myself for tomorrow." Ryan snatches his cap and promises to see them in the morning.

In the living room, underneath one of the mics, Lisa tells Trace, "I need a break. I have to get away from everything. After all that happened at the hospital, I'm tied up inside. Besides, I haven't slept for three days."

"That's not good. How about going to Five Islands Park in the morning? We could walk the beach. Maybe we could even kayak as we did as kids. Yeah?"

"I'd love it. Can we take a taxi? That way we can have drinks later and not worry about who's driving. What time were you considering?"

"Early, before the crowds, and yes, let's take a cab."

"Half past six? We could go to the park restaurant for breakfast and take a walk after."

The following morning, Lisa calls a cab. She and Trace take the elevator downstairs and wait outside for the ride to arrive. A weathered taxi pulls up next to them, and Trace yanks open the creaky door.

"Our destination is Five Islands Park, sir. The restaurant at the entrance."

"Okay. Buckle up."

Lisa looks at the belt and at Trace. She crinkles her mouth and reaches into her purse for a sanitizing wipe and, carefully, cleans the latch.

The driver gives dispatch the destination. "Which hotel?" A tinny voice replies with the name. "Okay, I'll go there after I drop this fare."

Nervous and preoccupied with their plans, Lisa taps her fingers on the seat. *What if Ryan's late? He's never late. I shouldn't worry. What if someone spots us?* She squints and looks out the back window but sees no familiar cars. *We're okay.*

The driver pulls to a hasty stop. "Twenty-eight dollars, sir. A little extra for the time of day."

Trace coughs. "Are you serious?"

"New rules, sir."

Not wanting to engage further, Lisa nods, and Trace hands over the cash. The cab drives off, and they step into the restaurant. Without pausing, the siblings proceed through the dining area, past the kitchen, and out the rear exit.

Lisa sighs with relief when she spots Ryan, who waits for them in a rented white Ford Explorer. The two slip into the backseat and duck low, behind the front headrests.

Trace teases, "Quite the get-up, Ryan."

"Hoodies are part of the dress code these days, and who can drive without sunglasses? You two ready?"

"All set."

Ryan drives away from the diner, and after ten minutes, he turns off the freeway to a service plaza, where he parks beside an air compressor. He darts to the back of the vehicle, replaces the license plate, and gets back into the SUV.

"What did you just do?" Trace asks.

"Changed the plate. The restaurant might have cameras, but it's unlikely there are any on the air compressor."

Trace chuckles. "You think of everything, my friend."

"I'm trying. We're now, officially, on our way. Next stop, Old Lyme, CT. Did you want to get upfront, Trace, before I hit the freeway?"

"Yep, I'll jump out now."

Once Trace sits in the front passenger's seat, Ryan points to the seatbelt. "You know, I grew up on the wrong side of the tracks. I've never been to the Old Lyme beaches." He shoves Trace. "I'm flying blind, so you lead the way."

"It's easy, but just in case, I'll get the GPS set up." He enters the address. "It will take an hour and forty-five minutes. Interstate ninety-five the whole way."

Lisa leans forward. "How about stopping for breakfast midway?"

Ryan smiles. "Hey, you know me. I'm ever ready for a meal. Let's do it."

CHAPTER 16

Twenty-first century challenges have left the quiet coastal town of Old Lyme untouched. On its streets, children play among historic homes and giant old oak trees. When Ryan exits the freeway and drives through the area, his eyes widen. "This is like something from a storybook. All joking aside, did Norman Rockwell live here?"

Trace laughs. "Buddy, wait until you see the shoreline. Take a right at the stop sign."

Ryan makes the turn and whistles. Clusters of little cottages with white picket fences span the distance. "I can only imagine what living here must be like in the summer."

Lisa scoots forward and pats him on the back. "It's amazing, right? We're just a few minutes from the highway, and yet we're in another world. In the summer, this area is bustling. Now, though, it's a quiet village."

"The second house on the left," Trace says. "That's what we're renting for the next two days."

Ryan parks, and Trace says, "I'll be back in a minute. I have to meet with the owner to sign for the keys."

Lisa exits the SUV and stretches. "Fresh air, sunshine, can't beat it."

"I can see why you two loved vacationing here. It had to be fun. Did you skateboard or surf?"

"We kayaked. Does that count? Mostly, I'd tag along. Trace was the adventurous one."

Trace returns and rattles the keys. The three head to the cottage, and Trace opens the door. "It's been vacant for a few weeks, so who knows what we'll find." He turns on the overhead fan to clear any dampness.

Lisa strolls over to the picture window and stares into the distance. "This is where Mom would sit. She'd crochet while we played in the sand. Once upon a time, I had quite a collection of tumbled rocks from the water's edge." She pauses and reminisces. "Sometimes, she'd let us hike to the pier to watch the fishermen. I remember chasing the seagulls that tried to steal the fish."

Ryan looks out over the Long Island Sound, where a fishing boat glides across the chop. "One of the reasons I loved Scouts was I got to do things others thought common because they had a father. I never had that experience. Didn't know my dad. Yours might be a criminal, but you had one."

"Yeah, we had one, but our experience was anything but ordinary." Trace knocks shoulders with his friend. "Our dad was rarely around, and when he was, we wished he wasn't."

Lisa looks at Trace and Ryan. "Come on, guys, let's figure out our next steps. Enough of dad talk."

Ryan smiles. "Tell me what to do, and I'm on it. Remember, I'm just the tailgate."

"See that island in the distance?" Trace points to a land mass with trees. "That's Fishers Island. In fact, we should leave for the ferry now. What do you recommend, sis?"

"We should go. I assume Father Kerry is the pastor at Our Lady of Miracles. It's the only Catholic Church on the island."

Back outside, they pile into the SUV, and Trace gives directions to the Fishers Island Ferry in New London, which lies about fourteen miles away. "You've never been in this area?"

Ryan shakes his head. "Nope. The furthest I've been in Connecticut is Killingworth, and that was for a Boy Scout camp."

"I remember that. We had fun, didn't we? Seems like I recall you catching a big trout in Deer Lake."

"My one and only."

Trace laughs. "Someday we should do that again. Since Mom grew up in Connecticut and has friends here, she'd visit whenever she could, which meant we got to come too. Once we're on the ferry, you'll get an ocean view of the coastline."

Lisa drifts in and out of their conversation, absorbed in her thoughts. While she stares out the window at the passing landscape, she remembers her mother's stories about growing up in the Old Lyme area. *Not much has changed since Mom was a kid. It's still a quiet, beautiful respite. Even has the same candy store, where she'd buy penny candy.* Lisa lowers her head. *She did the best she could, even trying to give us her experience.*

Ryan stops at an intersection, and a school bus drives past. Some of the children wave, and Lisa returns the gesture. Memories assail her. She recalls the sweetness of playing in the sand. *Trace's antics always made me laugh. He loved to toss a crab at me just to hear me scream.* She smiles, but then an unwanted memory intrudes, and her stomach tightens. She grips the window edge as, in her mind's eye, she watches her dad enter the cottage with a package wrapped in brown paper.

"This is a safe place," her mother had said. "I want to keep it that way. You can't bring your business in here."

Lisa's heartbeat races when she recalls her parents arguing. She'd hidden behind the sofa when the yelling began. Even now, sweat trails across her forehead when she re-experiences the fear she felt when the argument escalated. Then she sees it. Her father pushed her mother against the wall. "The emissary is on his way. The package will be gone in an hour." She feels her mother's terror, registers the way her mom holds her arms in front of her body, and Lisa knows the package held something terrible.

Her thoughts freeze as the car thump-thumps over a short bridge to the ferry landing. Hurriedly, Lisa wipes her eyes and takes a deep breath. *I can't get emotional. I must stay calm. There's too much at stake.* But she can't stop thinking about that package.

"We made it." Ryan announces. "From the looks of things, they're just beginning to load the ferry." He turns wide onto the platform and drives up to the ticket booth. "One car and three passengers." He hands the attendant a credit card. Once he's received the tickets, he passes them to Lisa and drives into a line with the other ferry traffic.

Lisa fingers the tickets and notices the instructions. "It looks like we have the choice of sitting in the car, strapped to our seats, or we can go up top and wander around. We can't do both. So, what do you two want to do? I'd love to go up top, but if you'd prefer to sit here, seatbelts on ..."

"Upper deck." Trace laughs. "No question. Follow me."

The ferry pulls away from the dock, and the trio watches the village cottages come into view. The playground near their cottage is absent of children. The only evidence of life comes from an older couple, who walk their dog on the beach. Lisa spots a blue building. "Look. Just like the one in the painting."

"No kidding." Trace stares. "You were right that the painting was a clue. It looks like the painter worked from a photo taken right here on this ferry. It's a leap, but I believe we're on the right path."

The mainland shoreline grows more distant, and the threesome weave through groups of passengers to the bow of the boat, where they can see the approaching island.

The moist wind sends Lisa's hair flying. She brushes it away from her face and tries—unsuccessfully—to knot it at the nape of her neck, now ruddy from the morning breeze. As the waves hit, the ferry rocks, and Lisa with it. She struggles to keep her balance. Ryan edges closer, and shoulder-to-shoulder with her, Ryan waves to the seagulls.

The ferry bumps against the dock buffers abruptly, and Ryan grabs Lisa when she staggers. She smiles, and his features light up.

An announcement sounds over the public address system: "All passengers need to return to their cars. Deboarding begins in ten minutes."

Trace leads the way down the stairs, and the three climb into the Explorer. Trace sits busy with the GPS, while Ryan focuses on Lisa through the rearview mirror. She sees his interest, grins broadly, and gives his shoulder a light pat. The two lock eyes and hold the moment.

"From my calculations—" Trace says, oblivious to the chemistry, "—the church should take us a short drive from the pier. Once we disembark, follow the main road to the center of town. I'll give block-by-block instructions after that."

Ryan pilots the SUV up the hill to a quaint town of small boutiques and specialty restaurants. At the main intersection, Trace tells Ryan to turn right. They steer through the narrow streets and into a thickly wooded area. Tucked into this forested haven sits an A-framed wooden structure with tall stained-glass windows, which face out to the ocean.

"Whoa, if I were to go to church, it would be to one like this," Ryan says as he parks the car.

"I remember coming here. I must have been about ten because Lisa was just a little tyke. For some reason, I thought angels lived inside the church. No idea why, but I sure could use an angel visit now."

They follow the stone-covered path to the chapel. The door swings open, and they step inside.

"Oh my gosh," Lisa exclaims. "Rainbows everywhere."

Trails of color pour through the stained glass and layer the interior of the church with pulsing light. The three of them stand and marvel at the sight.

Slowly, Lisa inhales and savors the magic. "No wonder Mom loved this place." She rubs a hand over the polished wooden pews and walks to the flickering candles beneath a large painting of Our Lady of Guadalupe. "Mom longed to visit the Basilica in Mexico City one day. Maybe we can help her make that dream a reality."

Trace recalls a childhood experience. His mom knelt by the candles. A warbler had gotten into the church, and it soared in and out of the refracted light. He smiles. *Now I know why I thought angels lived in this church.*

"Shall we find the priest?" Trace asks.

Lisa nods. "If he's here, I'm sure he'd be in the rectory. I saw it when we drove up. It's just to the side of the church."

They go back outside, retrace their steps to the rectory, and knock.

A slight man greets them and, with a strong Irish accent, says, "Can I help you?"

Trace holds out a hand, which the man shakes. "We're looking for Father Kerry. Is he available?"

"That would be me, my son. What can I do for you?"

"Father, I'm Trace Holmes, and this is my sister Lisa. Our mother, Katherine, asked us to come here and meet you. This is our friend, Ryan."

The priest studies the threesome. "How is Katherine?"

"She's in the hospital, Father, but she may be released in another week."

His lips tighten, and he questions them further, "What happened?"

"It's a long story, but she's recovering from a gunshot wound."

"And your father?"

"He passed away. An intruder murdered him."

"You're a Catholic?"

Lisa says, "We were raised Catholic, but I'm the only one practicing the faith."

"I see. Then you understand there are things a priest might know but can never reveal."

"Yes, Father."

"It would be wise for you to spend time with Our Lady. Katherine visited her frequently. You should do that as well."

Lisa looks at the priest's narrowed eyes and sees his seriousness. "I'll go there now, Father. Thank you."

They step away from the rectory, and Ryan says, "Strange conversation. Does anyone know what's going on?" He glances at Lisa.

"A priest cannot speak about anything said within the confessional. Whatever Mom shared in that setting is forever protected. But Father Kerry advised us to look at the image of Our Lady. There must be a reason."

Slowly, they walk back into the church and up to the painting.

Trace looks around. "What are we supposed to do?"

Lisa glances from one man to the other. "Let's sit and wait."

Ryan and Trace look at each other and raise their shoulders, confused.

Lisa kneels and studies the small altar. Candles line either side of the painting. In the middle of the altar, a raised antique bronze plaque explains the miracle of the image. Lisa tilts her head to the side and edges up to the altar. She fingers the plaque, which rests on a carved wooden stand about two inches high.

"Trace, could you come here?"

He gets up and stands by her side.

"Can you lift this plaque? Be careful."

He picks it up, but as he does so, the box lifts as well. Lisa studies the stand and sees that it isn't solid. It's a reliquary. "Hold still for a minute." She tugs a small tab on the underside of the wooden stand. It opens, and a small white box, taped securely and tied with wired string, falls into her hands. She inhales sharply and looks up at Trace with bulging eyes. "This is what we've been looking for."

Carefully, her brother returns the plaque to its original position and checks their surroundings before focusing on the white box. "Put it in your purse, and let's get out of here."

Lisa shoves the box inside her bag. "For some reason, I expected something bigger, maybe even heavy."

"So did I." Trace chews his top lip. "We all expected something tiny, but this is smaller than I anticipated. Whatever's inside, it has to be valuable—and dangerous."

The three leave the church and head straight to the SUV.

After putting on her seatbelt, Lisa says, "I'd sure like to know what's inside."

"Yeah, so would I, sis, but let's wait until we're on the ferry. I'd feel more at ease. Right now, I'm leery about what hides around the next corner."

Ryan starts the engine and checks his watch. "We've got some time if we're planning on the two o'clock ferry to New London. How about stopping at O'Rourke's Grill and Bar? It's just ahead. When we drove through town, I noticed they have outside seating in full view of the dock. What do you think? Yea or nay?"

"Okay by me." Trace turns to Lisa. "Stay close."

They walk to the restaurant and find seats outside. A ferry anchors at the dock.

Ryan startles and sits up straight. "Unbelievable. Isn't that Elena driving off the ferry? How could she have known? We were so careful."

Trace frowns. "That's something we won't solve right now, but what we will do is get on that return boat. We can't wait until two o'clock. Gather your things, fast."

Ryan mutters, "I think she's en-route to see Father Kerry. How is that possible? Who's with her?"

Trace and Lisa peer at the vehicle. Trace scowls. "I don't know but we'd best hustle. Let's go." After throwing down a tip, Trace says, "If we don't make this ride, we're in trouble. Come on. Now."

They reach the dock and drive onto the ferry deck without a moment to spare. Once they've parked behind the other travelers, Trace says, "That was a close one. We have a bit of a lead if they take the two o'clock ferry. But if they call for backup, we'll need help. Let's stay in the car, just to be cautious. Ryan, do you have a knife?"

"Yeah. Do you want to open the box?"

"Yes. We have a forty-five-minute ride ahead of us, and we need to know what we're dealing with."

Ryan digs into his pocket, pulls out his Scout knife, and hands it to Trace.

"Wow, this brings back memories. I don't even know where mine is." Slowly, Trace slices around the perimeter of the taped areas.

"Looks like you're performing surgery."

Trace ignores Ryan, and Lisa resists a smile.

"All right, the lid should be free now. You open it." He stretches to the back seat and hands the box to Lisa.

Slowly, she lifts the lid from the box. "There's a message taped to a cotton pad." She reads it out, "Take this to Professor Colin Boyle at the Metropolitan Museum of Art in New York City." Gingerly, Lisa peeks under the pad and gasps. Her hands tremble when she shows the guys.

Trace looks at Ryan and back at Lisa. "This has to be worth millions." Hundreds of brilliant diamonds, set in the shape of a star, glisten in the box. "We have to go to the police."

Ryan rubs his face. "Agreed. We can't do this on our own. This is way beyond our skill set."

They both turn and look at Lisa. "I know, I know. Just give me a few minutes. We can figure this out."

Trace's jaw muscles tighten. "We need a plan in place before we drive off this ferry. It's a matter of life and death. Are we clear on this point?"

"Yes. Let me do my thing for a few minutes. Have a little faith in me on this."

Trace grimaces and looks at Ryan before glancing back at Lisa. "Ten minutes. That's it. If we're not agreed on an alternative plan by then, we'll go straight to the police once we exit. This needs to end."

"All right. Thank you. Ten minutes it is."

Ryan turns the ignition key and rolls down the windows. An ocean breeze wafts through the cab as the ferry churns through the Long Island Sound toward the Connecticut mainland.

Every few minutes, Trace checks his watch. He runs a hand through his hair and taps on the dashboard. In contrast, Ryan watches Lisa through the rearview mirror. She closes her eyes and drifts into another world. After a few minutes, Lisa says, "We're unsure who to trust, but we believe the captain's a decent guy. So, we split up. The criminals know my Camry, and I suggest Ryan drives it and takes our tail on a wild ride. Eventually, he'll end up at the Met. Trace, you should drive the rental SUV and go straight to the police station. Ask to speak with the captain and explain everything. Ask if he and his officers could go to the Met with you. As for me, I'll call a cab and head to the Met as well. I'll find a way to Professor Boyle's office, and eventually, we'll meet up there. If all goes as planned, Boyle will have the treasure, the captain will have the criminals, and we'll get free and clear."

Trace's jaw juts, and he rubs his forehead. After a few moments of silent consideration, he purses his lips and glances over at Ryan. "Might work."

"It's dangerous, but I agree. Besides, I'd enjoy leading our trackers on a wild ride." A mischievous smirk creeps across his face.

The ferry reaches the dock and rocks to and fro. Ryan turns the key in the ignition. "Do we have any pressing reason to go back to the cottage now?"

Lisa shakes her head. "None I can think of."

Trace says, "Okay, so we drive back to the diner at Five Islands Park and return to the hotel."

For several minutes, they ride in silence.

Lisa clears her throat. "If I take a cab now, I can reach the Met by two o'clock. I don't need to go to the hotel. You could drop me off anywhere with access to taxis. The faster we act, the better for all of us."

"I don't like it. I'm worried about you." Trace studies his sister.

"Waiting only increases the risk."

"Probably."

"No, *absolutely*, it will increase the risk."

Ryan watches her in the rearview mirror. "What if I go with you? We both get in a cab. We both visit Professor Boyle. Who cares about giving chase to Elena and her partner? We'll deal with them later. I'm with Trace—I'm worried for you."

Each deep in thought, no one speaks.

Lisa wipes away a tear and stares at Ryan in the mirror. "I'd like it if we went together."

Ryan side-glances at Trace, who returns the look and tells Lisa, "I'm okay with the two of you going together. Ryan will make sure you're safe." He inhales slowly and tells Ryan to take the next exit. "The Southport train station is nearby, and there'll be cabs there. Let's do this."

Ryan makes the turn and pulls into the station parking lot. Three cabs wait for the incoming train to arrive.

Trace exits and speaks to one of the drivers. After a couple of minutes, he walks back to the SUV. "It's a go. The first cab will take you two to the museum. I'll drive the rental to the New Rochelle Police Station, and if all goes as planned, I'll join you within the hour."

CHAPTER 17

Lisa and Ryan climb into the back seat of a yellow taxi. Ryan says, "Metropolitan Museum of Art."

"Are we in a hurry today?"

"Yes, sir."

"I'll do my best." The cab driver speeds out of the parking lot and onto Interstate 95 south. "If the traffic's kind, we'll reach the museum in an hour."

"Thank you."

Ryan rests his hand on Lisa's. "How're you doing?"

"Okay. Better, now that you're traveling with me. It's been quite a journey. Sometimes it doesn't seem real—like I'll wake up soon. But, of course, that doesn't happen."

"I know I tease a lot, but I do it to lift some of the heaviness. I hope you don't think I'm minimizing your experience."

"Not at all, and I'm grateful for the levity. There's too little in our lives right now. What does surprise me are the memories that keep popping up. Like the ones at the cabin, or those at the beach, or even people's faces. Somehow, through these odd circumstances, the past has come alive again."

"That's a good thing." Ryan squeezes Lisa's hand. "Otherwise, how would you get through this mess?"

"True. I should feel grateful. How about you? How are you managing?"

"I like challenges, and Trace and I work well together, so—overall—I haven't minded the drama. But there's one surprising outcome."

"Yeah?"

"You and Trace, frequently, bring up your frustrations with your father. Some of the stories you've shared chill me. When I was younger, I envied Trace for having a dad. I never met Eric, and I don't recall seeing him at any games. But in my imagination, he was the embodiment of all things wonderful about a father. A dad I never had."

"And now you don't feel envious?"

"I might have had a healthier home life than you. I never experienced violence, and I can't think of a time I felt afraid."

Lisa leans over and kisses Ryan on the cheek. "Just because."

The cab jerks to an abrupt stop.

"We have a problem." The taxi driver has to raise his voice over the rising and falling wails of emergency vehicles. "There's an accident at Park and Eighty-First Street, and I can't budge. According to dispatch, this might be a long wait. You're two long blocks from the museum. If you want to walk it, I'll let you out here."

Ryan glances at Lisa. "We'll walk it." He pays the driver, and the two rush to the sidewalk. Because of the confusion ahead of them, they take an alternate route, down Eighty-Second Street. Ten minutes later, they stand in front of the Metropolitan Museum of Art.

"Stay close to me," Ryan says. "Let's race up the stairs." He grabs her hand, holds it tightly, and runs with her up the granite steps to the entrance. Her leather crossbody bag fits snugly between the two of them and keeps the treasure safe.

Ryan surveys the lines, and they head to the one closest to the entrance of the Egyptian collection. "Two tickets, please." He hands the clerk a credit card.

"Here you go, sir. Have a pleasant day."

With the tickets in hand, the two enter the museum and hurry to the nearby exhibit to look for a guide.

Lisa points to a woman speaking to a group of students. She wears a uniform and has an identification badge pinned to her bodice. "I suspect she's a docent. Shall we talk with her?"

"Let's do it."

Ryan waits for the woman to pause her monologue. "Excuse me, could you help us, please?"

"I'm just finishing here, so I'll be with you shortly."

Lisa and Ryan wait off to the side. A couple of minutes later, the docent walks over. "How can I help you?"

"It's a long story, but the condensed version is we need to meet with Professor Boyle. We have a gift for the museum—something he's waiting for."

"Very mysterious, but I need some exercise, so please, follow me." The woman leads them to a private elevator, which ascends to the fourth floor. The trio proceeds down two hallways to an area of multiple offices.

"Please wait here. I'll check to see if the professor's available."

When she walks away, Lisa looks into Ryan's eyes, and her lips tremble. "I'm scared."

"I'm anxious as well, but we're here, and everything is unfolding as we planned. It'll be okay. I promise."

When the docent returns, she raises her hands and shoulders. "I thought for sure Dr. Boyle would say no, but surprise, quite the opposite. He said he has five minutes he can spare. You'll need to talk fast. Follow me."

She takes them through a tall, intricately carved wooden door and down a narrow hallway to a high-ceilinged office, which overlooks New York City's Central Park. Lisa's eyes open wide when she swivels to look at the artifacts that adorn the room.

"You can have a seat here," the docent says.

Professor Boyle, an elderly gentleman with a nervous twitch, rises from his desk slowly and shuffles to them. His monocle hangs loose down his shirt and swings when he moves. "You have something for me?" He stammers. With pursed lips, he arches his brows while studying Lisa and Ryan.

"Yes, sir. We have a story that goes with it, but you need to see the item first."

Lisa reaches into her purse, pulls out the box, and gives it to the professor.

Boyle takes the packet and plods back to his desk. He sets the box on the polished walnut surface. Then, adjusting his monocle, he removes the lid with deliberate care. He holds up the folded paper and mouths the message while he reads. His face registers bafflement, and slowly, he lifts the cotton pad that covers the jewel.

Upon seeing the treasure, Boyle jerks backward and inhales sharply. He looks over at Ryan and Lisa in disbelief. "If this is what I imagine it to be, it's one of the crown jewels of Ireland—the Grand Masters Diamond Star. It disappeared in nineteen-oh-seven. There are many rumors about who confiscated it, but all efforts to find it failed."

The man's face grows ashen as he looks at Lisa and Ryan. "How did … where did … you find this?"

Lisa crosses her legs and rest her hands on her upper knee. "It's a complicated story, sir, but I'll share it if you want to hear."

While Lisa and Ryan meet with Dr. Boyle, Trace accompanies Captain Davis to the hospital. The two met privately at the station and concluded there must be a wiretap planted near Trace's mother. They walk into her room, and Trace calls out, "Hi, Mom. This will be a short visit, but I'll come back later. Captain Davis is with me, and he wants to check to make sure you're safe."

"I'm s-sure I am, son, b-but I'm happy for t-the visit."

"It will take just a couple of minutes, ma'am. Sorry to bother you."

The captain searches the area around the upper bed frame and dislodges a mic. After putting the device in his pocket, he proceeds to scour the remainder of the room and furniture.

"All done. Thank you, ma'am. We'll go on our way now."

"I'll see you later this evening." Trace blows a kiss as he leaves.

Once out of the room, the captain signals Trace to be careful of what he says. They enter the elevator and press the button for the basement. The captain leads the way to the hospital surveillance room. At a water dispenser, he fills a plastic cup, drops the mic into it, and turns to a technician, who sits in front of multiple screens.

"What's your name?"

"Raul, sir."

"Okay, Raul. We're dealing with a criminal case that's time sensitive. I need the footage of Room two-eleven for the last week. Can you pull it up?"

"Yes, sir."

"We'll sit and watch the comings and goings of people to and from that room."

The captain and Trace drag chairs closer to the monitors.

"Skip by medical staff and family. I'm looking for someone unexpected."

They watch as medical staff, cleaning staff, and family members zoom past their view.

Trace wrings his hands. "We're missing something. It has to be here."

"Let's give it a little more time. We haven't checked the midnight hours."

"Here's something." The tech points to a patient going into the room at one o'clock in the morning.

They watch as the psychologist goes into the room in his hospital gown. Furtively, he glances in all directions before entering. A minute later, he re-emerges.

"OMG. I have to get hold of Lisa." Trace pulls out his cell and taps in a message:

> *The shrink is the leak. He's the mastermind behind this mess. Be careful.*

They thank the tech and rush to the nurse's station on the second floor. The captain asks to see Dr. Schultz's medical file. He reads the concluding prognosis. "Surface shoulder wound. Released to the care of his primary physician." His face reddens. "Even his injury was a scam."

The captain calls his counterpart in Manhattan, tells him of the theft and the potential risk at the Metropolitan Museum of Art, and looks at Trace. "Captain Taylor will alert the Met security team, and even as we speak, NYPD police are moving in. There's one more action I need to take." He punches in a number. "Sergeant, mobilize the SWAT team and arrest Dr. Thomas Schultz." He listens and responds, "Yes, that's him. We have his home and office addresses on file. Be aware that he and his associates are armed and dangerous. I also need you to call the New London Police."

Trace listens while the captain tells the sergeant that Elena and her accomplice are on the two o'clock ferry. Davis gives a description of Elena and her vehicle and tells the officer to hurry.

To Trace, he says, "Ready?"

"Hell, yes."

"Let's get on the road. This is a showdown I don't want to miss."

At the police cruiser, the captain throws Trace a bulletproof vest. "Put this on. We're headed into battle."

The captain drives with sirens blaring. Trace sits white-knuckled while they careen through traffic and listen to police updates on the radio.

A text arrives from Lisa:

He's here.

Davis calls the NYPD captain. "The situation has escalated. We have a hostage situation."

With a grim expression, the captain maneuvers the cruiser through traffic. "I know you're worried, Trace, and you have a reason. But we have the guy trapped. Trust the system. He'll go down."

They listen to the radio communication from on-site and hear yelling between officers. "Shots fired. Shots fired."

"They'll move in now," the captain says. "They've crossed the line. I don't know Lisa well, but she's savvy. She'll figure out what to do."

"I wish I were there with her."

"And if you were, all of you would be dead. Witnesses don't survive crimes like this. Because you came to me, there's a chance everyone will leave alive."

They turn the corner and park on the sidewalk in front of the museum steps. The captain reaches into his glove compartment and retrieves his backup semi-automatic. "Take this and stay close. Put this police cap on. It's too big, but I don't want the officers to mistake you for the other side."

Together, they run up the steps. The police have built barricades to block civilians and the growing mass of reporters. Officers wave the captain in.

"What floor?"

"Fourth, sir. I'll lead the way." A young officer escorts them to a staff elevator. Inside, the young man presses the floor button, while the captain adjusts his vest. The lift rises with soft judders. When it stops, the back door of the elevator opens. The three men hurry down the hallway. Gunfire erupts.

"Get behind me and stay there," the captain yells to Trace.

With guns in hand, the police officers approach the SWAT team.

"Status?" the captain asks.

"Hostages are at gunpoint, sir. They've threatened to kill them, one at a time, if conditions aren't met."

Sudden chaos flares. The abductors shout, and the hostages scream. The SWAT team seizes the opportunity and charges. Captain Davis moves in with them. Multiple shots echo through the building. Not sure what's happening, Trace doesn't know what to do. Then Lisa calls his name.

"Over here." Lisa and Ryan crouch behind an executive desk, and Trace rushes to join them.

"I felt so scared you'd be harmed." Trace wraps his arms around each of them.

"We would have been—" Ryan says, "—if not for Lisa. She pretended to faint to cause a distraction. Right then, the SWAT team stormed in. We ducked behind Boyle's desk."

"Where is Boyle?" Trace asks.

"I, ah, I don't know. I thought he was beside us." Ryan spots him and points. "There he is." Boyle crouches behind a medieval chest and clutches the box with the jewel.

"Thank God, you're all safe," Trace says.

The trio watches as multiple emergency personnel rush into the room. Two bodies lie on the floor. Schultz and an older man. The medical team administers aid to both men, but finally cover the older man with a white cloth.

They focus on Schultz and work to stop the hemorrhaging. Seeing that he's alive, Lisa stands and marches to the therapist. "What are you doing? Get back here," Trace cries out.

Determined, Lisa ignores her brother and the officers' warnings to stay back. Angry, she stands with hands at her hips and watches the medics work on Schultz. Her eyes meet his, and even with his substantial injuries, the man appears alert. "I trusted you, but you used me. People are dead because of you."

Captain Davis grips Lisa's arm and pulls her away. "I'm with you, ma'am, and I'd like nothing better than to shoot the little—, but we have to back off and follow protocol."

Lisa looks up at the imposing officer and trembles uncontrollably. Overcome, she embraces Davis and holds him tightly while she sobs.

Awkwardly, the captain pats her on the back and says, "It'll be okay. I'll make sure of it." He motions to one of his officers.

"Yes, sir?"

"Take these three civilians to the station so they can retrieve their transport. Can I depend on you to do that?"

"Yes, sir. You can count on me."

"All right, Officer Chen. I expect a call once they're safely in their own vehicle."

"You'll hear from me shortly, sir."

The captain motions to the group of three to follow the officer. "You're going home."

CHAPTER 18

Trace sits in the front seat of the patrol car, and a steel mesh cage separates him from Lisa and Ryan. He glances back at the two and concludes the cramped vinyl seats hold two lovers, who don't mind the spartan ride.

"Friends of yours?"

"One is. The other's my sister."

"Ahh, you're okay with that?"

"Yeah, he's been a friend since high school."

"How did you get messed up in all this?"

"That's a long story, but it goes back to my dad. He was no good."

"Sorry about that."

Vacantly, Trace stares at the apartment buildings and high-rise structures as they zoom past. On the two-way radio, dispatch announces traffic problems, altercations, and fires. A message from Captain Davis broadcasts, "To all who provided assistance at the Met, well done. The operation was a success because of you." The officer glances at Trace and, through the rearview mirror, at Lisa and Ryan.

"Thank you for responding as you did, officer. We've been through hell and back, and finally, there's an end in sight."

Another message airs from dispatch, "Reporters and TV crews block the station entrance. We've mobilized the PR team to handle the swarm. Use side or back entryways."

The officer makes a hasty turn onto an alternate road. "The press will want to talk with you. In my experience, they'll stop at nothing to get a story."

Trace straightens. "What should we do?"

"Avoid them if you can. They're merciless. I'll take you to the side entrance. From what I can see, they haven't covered that access yet."

He parks at the side of the building, next to a concrete-block structure. "I don't know where your vehicle's parked, but you have a fighting chance from here."

"This is perfect, officer. Our SUV's in the back lot. We can weave through the cars and avoid the chaos. Thanks for all your help."

Trace climbs out of the patrol car, reaches for the officer's hand, and shakes it repeatedly. "I don't know what we would have done without your skill."

Ryan and Lisa follow Trace's lead and thank the officer.

Slowly and in silence, the three walk on the black pavement and approach the rental SUV, where they duck behind vehicles to avoid attention.

"You have the keys," Ryan says to Trace. "Do you want to drive?"

"Sure. You want to sit in the backseat with my sister?"

"Maybe."

"When do you need to return the rental?"

"Tomorrow morning."

"Hmm. Okay."

Trace pulls out of the parking lot and uses the alternate road down which the officer brought them. He checks the rearview mirror. Ryan sits with his arm wrapped around Lisa's shoulders, and her head rests against his chest. A relieved smile crosses Trace's face, and he reaches for the radio nob to select instrumental music.

En route to the hotel, Trace reviews the events of the day. The mic at his mother's hospital bed. The stolen jewel. The confrontation at the museum. He grips the steering wheel, and his knuckles whiten. *I must protect my family.*

As an extra precaution, Trace parks the car near the rear entrance of the hotel. A glance at Ryan and Lisa brings a fresh smile. They've fallen asleep.

"Hey, you two, we're here."

Lisa stirs and laughs in surprise. "I must have been exhausted."

Ryan lifts his arm from Lisa. "Ditto."

They gather their belongings, head into the hotel, and wait for the elevator.

In the lift, Ryan says, "There's nothing like tagging along with the Holmes kids. Each day's a workout."

Trace gives him a playful nudge. "You said you were bored at work."

"Touché."

At their suite, Trace unlocks the door. "Should we order in for dinner?"

"Sounds good." Ryan rubs his abdomen.

"Let's go for something substantial. We deserve it," Lisa says.

Trace retrieves his cell. "I'll have prime rib, with all the sides. I'm starving—haven't eaten since breakfast."

"Make that two. Medium-well for me," Ryan says.

Lisa chuckles. "Hmm. You're right. I'll have a salmon steak with fresh vegetables, big brother."

"All right, I'll call in the order."

Trace startles when his phone rings.

"Hello, Captain."

"Mr. Holmes. You got back all right?"

"Yes, thank you. We're in our suite now."

"Good. I have concerning news for you all."

Trace's face falls. "I'm putting you on speaker."

The three listen to the captain. "When Trace told me about the mics, I knew they came from us. We're the only entity with access to your suite. My men tracked the mics back to one of our techs. They feed into our system, but through an encrypted pathway. Only this technician had access, and we have him in custody. While we were busy in New York City, my people interrogated him. It turns out this man had two jobs. He worked for us and Schultz.

"You were right to doubt our force. Your conclusions were off, but because of your doubts, we've solved a long-standing mystery. This guy has compromised our work with several high-profile cases, not just yours. Wiretapping, illegal surveillance—he'll face prison time."

Lisa says, "How did he get involved with Schultz?"

"I don't have the details as yet, but my men are at Schultz's home now. From what they've reported, we've uncovered a major trafficking operation. Our tech was part of that."

Lisa gasps. "What about my dad? Was he part of this too?"

"We don't have all the facts, so don't jump to conclusions, but from what I can deduce, Schultz used your father. I assume the FBI did, too. The late Mr. Holmes made for an easy mark. He had the cover they needed, he was cunning, and he traveled internationally. However, somewhere along the line, things turned, and he couldn't extricate himself. The network went after him. Don't get me wrong, he wasn't innocent, and had he lived, we would have prosecuted him. That said, he might not have been the monster you fear him to have been."

Trace asks, "What about the jewel? How does that fit in?"

"My information is preliminary at this point, but the situation involves an arrangement between a New York City magnate and Schultz. The NYPD and our office are working together on the case. Once I'm confident of the details, I'll let you know."

"Thank you, sir. We appreciate the update."

"Don't get too excited. It's not over yet. The FBI's waiting on the sidelines. They may be quiet now, but they haven't forgotten us."

When Trace finishes the call, he looks at Ryan and Lisa. "Not forgotten us? What does that mean?"

Playfully, Ryan says, "I don't know but let's get rid of the mics."

CHAPTER 19

While Trace watches the sunrise from his bedroom window, he stretches. The treetops sparkle with the morning dew, and a bald eagle soars past and perches amid the branches. A feeling of contentment settles over him. The aroma of brewing coffee reaches him, and he strolls into the kitchen, where Ryan stands at the coffee pot.

"Didn't know you spent the night."

"Does that bother you?"

"Heck no. Just adds an interesting dimension to our friendship."

Ryan takes a sip of coffee. "Do you have plans for the day? I'm open to anything, but I need to return the rental."

"I'll go with you. Otherwise, after yesterday's revelations about Dad, I'd like to visit the house. This time, my interest isn't in the mess. I want to piece together what happened in plain sight. After that, we should go to the storage unit."

"Did you tell the captain about that?"

"No, but I should."

"My thoughts, too. This complicated situation will get messier with both the FBI and the police digging into the case. Why not call Captain Davis before we head out?"

"Kinda dread it, but you're right. I'll do that now." Trace punches in the captain's number.

"Trace?"

"Yes, sir."

"What's up?"

"I need to talk with you about something serious. Can I meet you for breakfast?"

"You're a man after my own heart. Name the place, and I'll be there."

"How about George's Diner in Ossining in an hour?"

"Sounds good."

Trace disconnects and glances at Ryan, who asks, "Should we all go, or do you want to go alone?"

"Let's all go. We're in this together, and afterward, we can head to the house."

"Okay. We need to return the rental first and then come back for Lisa before we drive to Ossining."

Trace says, "I'll leave her a note to explain the plan."

When they leave, the door slams and awakens Lisa. She startles and sits up in bed. After peeking around the bedroom door, she realizes she's alone. Fresh coffee entices her into the kitchen, where she finds a note.

We'll be right back. Returning the rental.

After a few sips of brew, she heads to the bathroom to take a shower. Roughly ten minutes later, Lisa sits on the deck, set for the day, and Trace and Ryan return.

Trace teases, "Sleeping beauty has arisen."

"Stop that." Lisa chuckles. "What have you been up to?"

Ryan smiles. "I returned the rental, and now we're planning to meet the captain for breakfast."

"Me too?" She looks at Trace.

"Of course. We need to leave now, are you ready?"

"All set."

The three of them collect their belongings and head out to the parking lot. The drive takes thirty minutes, and they enter George's Diner and find a table off to the side, which overlooks the Hudson River. They order coffees and check out the specials on the chalkboard.

A few minutes later, the captain swaggers in. "Sorry about that, guys. I had a calamity I needed to manage before I could take off. Have you ordered?" He positions a chair at the end of the table, where he has more room and can see each of them.

Lisa shakes her head. "No, just coffee."

The server comes to take their orders. Once she leaves, the captain straightens his chair and looks right at them. "All right, let's get on with it. Tell me what's so pressing."

He observes Lisa's red-rimmed eyes and Trace's clenched jaw. Ryan taps on the tabletop and looks at no one and everyone.

"You wouldn't ask to meet here if this wasn't serious. From the look of things, you're in deep and don't know how to get out."

Trace nods. "Yes, sir. We trust you but not the FBI. You know we've done our own investigating."

"And now you're realizing that can be dangerous."

"Correct. We discovered our father had a cabin not far from here." Trace lowers his voice. "We drove there and found boxes of papers, bank documents, treasury notes, and stacks of hundred-dollar bills. We packed as much as possible into our trunk and put it in a storage unit here in Ossining."

The captain puckers his lips and looks at each of them. "You have my attention."

"Maps of different countries cover the inside walls of the cabin with some cities circled."

The captain rubs the side of his face and appears deep in thought. "I don't have jurisdiction in that area; however, since I'm investigating your father, who lived in my jurisdiction, I could call the Putnam Valley police to ask for an assist."

He exhales loudly. "This is something that can't wait. You're targets. I know the FBI well enough to realize they'll have a tail on you." He rubs a hand across his mouth and stares at the table.

Lisa asks, "What can we do? Please, help us."

Captain Davis weighs his options and says, "Let's check out the storage unit. I need to see what we're dealing with. In a couple of minutes, and I'll tell you *when*, you will exit through the back of this diner. You'll climb into my SUV. The windows are dark, so you're protected. Before I do that, though, there's something else I must do. Wait here for me."

He pushes his chair back and walks over to a table where a young couple sits. At the captain's approach, they sit up straight.

The captain clears his throat. "Would you two help me?"

"Anything, sir."

"My friends and I are about to leave. An urgent matter has come up. Are you interested in free breakfasts, tips included?" He shows them the cash, and they stand and follow him over to the group's table.

Captain Davis says, "See you three in a minute."

Trace, Lisa, and Ryan recognize the signal, say "hello" to the couple, and leave via the back of the restaurant. The captain waits for them. Once inside the patrol cruiser, Trace gives directions to the storage unit.

The captain shakes his head. "In my entire career, I haven't had a case like yours. If you ever get tired of your jobs, let me know. I just might hire you as investigators."

Minutes later, they pull into the storage area, and Trace indicates their unit. Captain Davis parks next to the container, and Trace gets out and unlocks the roll-down gate. The captain strolls inside and searches through a few of the boxes. Alarmed, he stands tall and faces the three. "You're playing with fire. You don't know what you're dealing with. Move these boxes into my cargo area, now. We have to get this out of here and fast."

Trace, Ryan, and Lisa whisk away as many of the boxes as will fit in the back of the captain's SUV and close up the container.

"Come on, come on," the captain says, impatient. "Get in."

He speeds away from the storage unit and calls for backup. Davis gives instructions for patrol cars to cover every onramp of the Sprain Brook Parkway south. "Clear the freeway," he commands. As soon as he reaches the Parkway, he sounds the sirens.

"What's going on?" Lisa asks, confused by the alarm and the call for backup.

"Those documents you found contain information that implicates the FBI. You've discovered the mother lode. That's why the Feds came after you. Somehow, they learned your father had the information. They want it, and frankly, they'll silence anyone who knows about it."

Lisa blanches. "But why would Dad have it?"

"My guess? Protection. Maybe he planned to bargain with it. Maybe he planned on selling the information. I don't know, but all hell's going to break loose. Make sure you have your seat belts on tight."

The captain accelerates to ninety miles an hour. Patrol cars sit at various ramps, lights flaring. Trace grips the handle above the window and holds on with all his strength. Lisa and Ryan duck down and hold onto each other.

The captain says to Trace, "Take the weapon out of the glove compartment and prepare to use it. This is about to become an intense ride."

A helicopter gives chase and dips low. "Stop your vehicle. Pull over. Stop your vehicle."

The captain presses down on the accelerator pedal. "If we stop, we're dead."

Ryan tightens his hold on Lisa when the increased speed makes the cruiser shake.

The captain rings his front desk, "Call NYPD and ask for air assist. I need coverage. Got a chopper on my tail."

Within minutes an NYPD helicopter hovers above them. The other chopper turns away.

"We have a chance now," the captain says. "Slim, but a chance."

He calls the station again, "The FBI will arrive soon. Alert the team. This is not a friendly visit. I repeat, this is not a friendly visit. Contact the fire department and tell them to bring in their trucks. I'm five minutes away. Once I drive in, close the entrances with the trucks. Get hold of the media and make sure they can get on site."

Tires screeching, the captain drives into the station lot. After him, the fire trucks arrive and proceed to block the exit.

"We've got to move quickly." The captain sets the parking brake. "Fetch a box each from the back of the vehicle and get inside."

Lisa, Trace, and Ryan move as fast as they can. Two officers run out to help them with the crates.

Once inside, the captain exhales and motions for the three to follow him to a back room. He shouts toward the front desk, "You know nothing. Keep saying that. You didn't see anything, and you know nothing."

He turns to the three. "Any of you tech-savvy?"

Ryan raises his hand. "I am."

"Okay, give me something to brag about. Get this stuff into digital format. I saw a few thumb drives in the boxes. When you find them, give them to me, and I'll put them in the safe. You're in charge now, Ryan. Make these guys work. We only have a few minutes."

Lisa finds the thumb drives. "Captain, you wanted the USB Flash drives. I have several, sir."

Captain Davis calls in an officer. "Teal, take these drives and store them in the safe. Add these gold certificates and bonds as well. When you finish, work with Frankl and secure these two boxes of cash with the other items. Make sure all of it's locked up. No Mistakes. You have a couple of minutes. Move it."

"Yes, sir. I'm on it."

Ryan feeds a stack of papers into a large scanner. Trace follows his lead and does the same at another scanner. After finishing, they put the papers back into the box and set it to one side.

The captain gives Ryan a container of unused flash drives. "Download what you've digitized and make multiple copies. Hurry. Give them to me as soon as you're done."

Trace and Ryan load the thumb drives and pass them to the captain.

"We're in business." The captain pockets two of the drives and tells Officer Teal to store the rest of them in the safe with the others.

Davis strides to the two front-desk officers and gives each a flash drive. "When I open the door, slip these to reporters Nelson and Smith. They've always been good to us. Make sure no one sees."

Outside the station, sirens blare and vibrations rumble as the police helicopter circles. The local reporters broadcast the event on live television and demand explanations. Inside the station, officers watch on multiple screens and see the FBI's arrival.

A heavily armed squadron marches through the crowd and to the entrance of the New Rochelle Police Station. The lead agent announces their arrival, "FBI. Open the door immediately."

"Everyone in their places," Captain Davis calls out and gives the okay to unlock the doors.

FBI agents barge in and take hold of the captain. "You will pay for this mess," the lead agent mutters. "Where are the documents?"

Davis motions to his office. "Behind my desk."

The agents march into his office and locate the boxes. After a quick check for content, they carry the cargo outside.

The front-desk officers slip a flash drive into the hand of each of the two named journalists. Though they don't speak, their eyes communicate for them. The reporters nod, pocket the drives, and leave with their teams.

"We have the three conspirators, sir," an agent yells out. "Shall I put them in the prisoner transport van?"

"Cuff them. We'll take them out to the van once we have everything in place."

Agents grab Lisa, Trace, and Ryan, and yell at them to sit on the floor, their backs against the wall. They slip zip ties on their wrists. Lisa sits in shock and stares into the distance.

Through the doorway, FBI agents hold back the police at gunpoint. The captain stands with his hands raised, and agents point their guns at him. Heavy pounding sounds at the station's front door, and reporters demand access. All the while, sirens blare outside.

An officer, positioned behind a glass barrier at the front desk, eases her hand to a control panel and presses a button. The television monitor shouts out: *Breaking News. Breaking News.*

Everyone turns and focuses on the monitor. Images of the FBI raiding the police station, as well as footage of the chaos, go national. A correspondent announces, "We've secured evidence of FBI involvement in an international scheme to take down specific foreign leaders. Our initial review implicates top D.C. officials."

"What the hell?" The lead FBI agent turns to the captain. "I will deal with you personally, Davis. This is not over." To his men, he gives the order, "Pack up. We're out of here."

CHAPTER 28

In an attempt to get comfortable on the cold laminate floor, Lisa shifts her position. The zip ties dig into her wrists, and any movement sends runners of pain up her arm. Ryan struggles to inch nearer to her. His voice cracks when he asks if she's okay. When the FBI agents hurry out of the building, Trace shouts, "Officers, we need help."

An officer comes to them and cuts the ties. "Are you all okay?"

Trace looks at Lisa. "We will be. We just need a few minutes."

Lisa brings her hands to her face and sobs. The captain comes in and sees her distress. "Guys, I'm sorry you had to go through this. But now you know what you're up against. They won't stop until they get what they want, or they recreate an acceptable story."

"What do you mean?" Lisa asks.

"They'll create a different narrative, make it convincing with conjured evidence, and will wait for the storm to pass."

"What do you think will happen?" Trace stares at Davis.

"Because of their exposure, the D.C. folks will act fast to create an alternate narrative that makes them the good guys. The public may question it, but they'll go on with their lives. People like us will either accept the story or get eliminated. This is a poker game with real people. You make choices."

Ryan says, "Sounds ominous."

"Realistic." The captain turns and surveys the three of them. "You need to take all precautions. Agreed?"

"Yes, sir."

The captain motions for one of his sergeants to approach. "Officer Simpson, drive these civilians to Ossining. George's Diner. They need to retrieve their vehicle."

"Yes, sir."

The officer leads the three through the side exit and to her patrol car. "We'll have to improvise," she says. "Two in the back and one in front."

Trace settles into the front seat and introduces himself. "We're grateful for your help. It's been quite the day."

"I can see that. When I went through training, I had no idea what I was getting into. One crazy situation after another." She grins. "You can call me Becca."

The officer turns onto the freeway and side-glances at Trace. "You have a nickname. Did you know that?"

"No. I hope it's not bad."

"Nah. The officers call the three of you *The Sherlocks*."

"Ha."

Everyone chuckles and relaxes. Becca confides, "I grew up in New Rochelle and even went to the same high school as you." She nods at Trace. The two share stories about those years and laugh about a fleeting encounter at a party.

"Now look at us," Becca says. "I'm a police officer, and you're a businessman. Who could have imagined a shy girl like me and a football star like you would, someday, ride in a patrol car together?"

By the time they reach George's Diner, Becca and Trace have stopped listening to the dispatch communiques. They've found a friend in each other.

"Hey, guys," Ryan says. "We have an audience." He climbs out of the patrol car and waves wildly to the customers in the diner, who stare out the windows.

"Come on, Lisa. Join in." He grabs her hand and swings her around.

"I swear you're a nutcase."

"Nah, just offering them a show and having some fun. They mustn't appreciate it though."

Lisa follows his gaze. The patrons have focused on their meals again. Ryan gives Lisa a sly smile.

Officer Becca laughs. "I'm going to share this story back at the station."

Trace lingers as they say goodbye. "Would you consider continuing this conversation at another time? Over dinner, perhaps?"

"I'd like that. Here's my card. I'm always reachable at that number."

With a smile, Trace pockets the card. "I'll call soon."

Ryan and Lisa smile and walk into the diner. Ryan grabs a booth with high sides. "Do you suppose we can order a meal and actually eat it?" His mischievous grin sets them off laughing.

A server approaches, and her eyes widen. "I remember you."

"You do?" Lisa asks.

"Of course. You came in this morning and gave your table to a couple and left. That was quite the gift. They ate all four orders. You made their day. Was it their anniversary?"

Lisa shrugs. "Something like that. We wanted to surprise them."

"Well, you did. Now, how may I help you fine folks?"

Ryan says, "I'll go with your burger special and all the trimmings, plenty of fries, and a tall beer on tap."

"I'll have the same as my buddy." Trace hands over the menu.

"And you, ma'am?"

"Hmm, I'll have your chicken salad and a tall unsweetened iced tea." Lisa pauses for a moment and adds, "And we'll each have a slice of cheesecake for dessert."

"Now we're talking." Ryan chuckles.

Once the server leaves, Lisa turns to Trace. "Didn't we leave some boxes in the storage unit?"

Her brother studies her. "We did. There wasn't enough room in the captain's car. We'll pick up the remainder after lunch and close out the unit."

Trace's cell phone pings. Lisa leans in to read the message. The text comes from the captain. "I'm almost afraid to read this."

I've contacted the Putnam Valley police. They will meet with my men at the cabin in another hour. You three stay clear.

Trace texts a reply:

No worries. We're at the diner, enjoying a hamburger on you.

The captain replies:

Without me? I'll have to take a rain check, LOL.

Trace laughs. "He's a good sport. It took us a while to trust him, but he's got my admiration. The guy hung in there with us even when all hell broke loose."

After their meal, they return to the storage unit. Trace unlocks and lifts the rollup door. Only two boxes remain. "I'll put them in the trunk and will turn in the keys. Meet me in front of the office."

After the trunk slams shut, Lisa starts the engine and waits for Trace at the front of the main building. A few minutes later, he steps out, hands in the air. "Free at last."

Lisa grins. "You're too funny. Unless anyone objects, I'm driving to the house."

"It's your car. You're in charge."

"What power. To the house we go." Lisa turns onto the freeway. After a few minutes, she says, "Do you think we could surprise Mom with the kind of home she's always wanted?"

"Yeah. We should toss the mismatched furniture Dad insisted she purchase secondhand. Oh, and those beds he found on special at the warehouse. And how about the table that was on sale at Goodwill? I was with him for that bargain." Trace snorts.

Lisa rubs a thumb across her lower lip. "Dump it all. Let's begin afresh. A new home. A new life."

Ryan and Lisa exchange a smile through the mirror, and he offers a thumbs-up.

Lisa taps on the steering wheel. "Yep, let's have some fun."

"I'm all in. New furniture it is. When we last visited, the painters had almost finished the front room. If the floors are ready, we can go shopping."

Trace's cell rings. "It's the captain again." He darts a glance at Lisa and Ryan and puts the call on speaker.

"Hello, sir."

"Trace. Where are you?"

"We're driving to the house now. I've put you on speaker."

The captain says, "I just received word that Dr. Thomas Schultz passed in his sleep last night. There's been no statement about the cause of death."

"You suspect foul play?" Lisa asks.

"Yes, but I'm hesitant about tackling this mystery. Had the guy survived, he would have spent the rest of his life in jail. Someone wanted to make sure he wouldn't talk."

"Which is why you're telling us?"

"Yes and no. I wanted you to know he's no longer a problem. I also wanted you to hear how these people take care of loose ends."

Trace frowns. "Lesson learned, sir. Thank you."

"Remember, you still owe me a meal. Soon, I plan to collect." Davis chuckles.

Lisa grins. "We look forward to it."

At the house, Lisa steers onto the driveway. Gone are the cars for the drywall repairmen, the painters, and the police officers. Only the dumpster remains, and it sits squarely in the middle of the driveway, close to the house. She parks behind it.

Once out of the car, the group stands and studies the building.

"Lots of memories here," Lisa says. "But something's different."

"Someone's mowed the grass and trimmed the hedges," Trace says. "Did either of you arrange for a gardener?"

Lisa and Ryan shake their heads.

"There's a new security door at the entrance. And the windows have new wood blinds. You didn't arrange for any of this, Lisa?"

"No, I didn't even think to do so."

At the front door, Lisa does a double take and stares at her brother. "Remember the broken clay pot that sat here?"

"Yeah."

She points to a Talavera planter with white daisies, which now sits at the door. "Someone who knows Mom well put this here."

They step inside. The furniture is gone. The scattered wall hangings now rest neatly in a corner, stacked carefully one upon the other. Only one painting hangs on the wall, suspended above the fireplace. Neither Trace nor Lisa has seen this seascape before. They stand beneath it and ponder where it might have come from.

Ryan joins them. "Wow. That's beautiful. Someone must have commissioned this. Think about it, a mother with two boys and a daughter sitting on a grassy knoll watching the seagulls in the sky. The older boy has brown skin, and the other two children have white. Yep, commissioned."

Dumbfounded, Lisa and Trace stare at each other.

"Let's see if anything's written on the back." Trace removes the painting from the wall and checks for identifying information. Lisa watches from the side. A small label reads: *To my love*.

Lisa says, "Whoa, that's tender. Not something Dad would write. But who could it be?"

"I might have an idea, but right now, I'm off to check the dumpster to see if the old furniture's there." Trace walks outside, and leaves Lisa mulling over who could have written the loving message. She follows her brother and, together, they climb the side of the dumpster and peer into the container. As expected, the household furniture fills the receptacle—gutted couches, broken chairs, and old mattresses. Lisa stares at the tangled pieces of the home she once knew and wonders if the neighbors pitched in to help.

Back in the house, Lisa raises her hands, perplexed. "This is so strange. The captain didn't mention anything about the furniture, did he?"

"No, and I'm certain he had nothing to do with this. Let's check out the rest of the house. Pick a room and see what you can find." Trace strides away.

Ryan goes to the bedrooms. "The only furniture here is bed frames and dressers. Whoever cleared the house knew what they were doing."

"And saved us a lot of hassle." Lisa walks over to the back door and looks out at the yard.

"I don't believe it. Trace, come here. Our Secret Santa got rid of the old rusty swing set with the dangling chains. Now there's a picnic table with built-in benches in its place."

"I'll be." Trace points to the old doghouse. "Our Santa must have painted it. Do you remember our cocker spaniel?" He smiles at Lisa. "Dad hated that dog, but it sure brought a lot of joy to the rest of us."

"Whoever did all this, knows us. What the heck? I'm checking the basement. I want to see if this mystery person tackled that mess too."

Lisa eases down the creaky wooden steps and pauses, stunned by what she observes. Someone's fixed the dangling light bulb to the ceiling and encased it in a glass dome shade. A new washer and dryer occupy the far wall. And next to the appliances, a laundry basket holds clean, folded clothes. Someone washed the dirty clothes.

Our unknown person must love Mom because he or she wants to make her daily life easier for her. Lisa weeps and sits on the steps. At first, soft, quiet tears erupt, but then deep, wrenching, exhausted sobs spill from her soul. When she goes back upstairs, she finds Trace and Ryan in the kitchen, opening cabinets and pulling out drawers.

"Mom's got new dishes and silverware." Trace beams.

"New pots and pans as well." Ryan adds. When he turns and looks at Lisa, his smile fades. "You okay?"

"This is overwhelming, is all." Lisa wipes away a tear. "Whoever's done this loves Mom dearly."

Trace takes out his cell and snaps pictures. "She'll enjoy seeing all the improvements. Who knows, we may need these pics for reference when we purchase the new furniture."

Lisa wanders out of the front exit. Ryan joins her and wraps his arm around her waist. Together, they look at the neighborhood and, finally, at each other. After a deep breath, Lisa falls into his arms, where she rests.

Trace walks outside and clears his throat. "Sorry to interrupt. Are we ready to head back to the hotel?"

"Yes. We finished what we came here to do. Why don't you drive?" Lisa says. "Ryan and I have a few things to discuss."

"I bet you do." Trace takes the keys. "All aboard."

A neighbor spots them and hurries over. "How's it going?"

"It's been a tough couple of weeks, but Mom's doing much better. Thank you for asking. We hope she'll come home within the week. Once she gets settled, we can relax."

"Your family's been through a lot. Everyone on the street is rooting for you. We've taken up a collection and offer it as a help toward all the repairs. I know you had friends work on the inside of the house, but a couple of us worked on the yard. We're here for you." The middle-aged man hands Trace an envelope.

"I don't know what to say except thank you so much." He reaches for the neighbor's hand, but the man shoulder hugs him instead.

"Take care now."

Trace watches the neighbor walk away. The man's kindness leaves Lisa and her brother wiping away tears. The trio climbs into the car, and Trace starts the engine and backs out of the driveway. On the way to the hotel, a call comes in from the captain. The vehicle speaker broadcasts the call.

"Hey, Captain. What's up?"

"We've been working on the digitalized documents you retrieved from the cabin. There's plenty of incriminating information tied to the FBI, and you should stay clear of that. But there are a few documents that belong to your family. And there's the question of the money."

"What do you mean, the money?"

"Let's meet Friday. I have a few things to show you. Does ten in the morning work?"

"My calendar's open. Should Lisa come as well?"

"Of course. This is a family affair."

"I'll see you Friday."

CHAPTER 21

Laughter and shrieks of delight resound in the once-somber hotel suite. Lisa and Ryan play tag in their swimsuits before taking the elevator to the rooftop pool. They beg Trace to come with them, but he chooses solitude.

"You two go and have fun. I've work I need to do."

"Come on. Forget all that stuff for a while."

"I'll play with the idea, okay? Maybe a little later."

After the door closes, Trace looks across the room—home for the last couple of weeks—and realizes how much he misses his childhood abode. Without a second consideration, he'd trade this luxury accommodation for his modest nine-by-ten-foot bedroom. *Life at home may not have been the best, but it was home, and that's where I want to be. Home.*

Two boxes sit on the floor beside his bare feet. The remnants from the storage unit. Trace stares at them and clenches his teeth. One more thing he needs to do. After picking up one of the boxes, he sets it on the couch beside him, determined to go through the contents and bring some sort of closure to his father's iniquities. Trace takes a sip from his can of soda and prepares for what he might find.

Sheet by sheet, he reviews the papers and puts them in one of two piles—family or police. The latter grows exponentially as the noon sun shifts on its daily trajectory. Travel bills, invoices for hotels, spreadsheets, and lists of people—so much stuff it makes for a sobering task, but Trace keeps a rein on his emotions—until he finds a handwritten letter addressed to Katherine. He sets it aside for when he finishes sorting the papers.

An hour later, he stares at the stack he'll give to the captain—fragments of a hidden life that destroyed the family. When he thinks about that sordid world, Trace cringes. *I'll give Mom and Lisa what Dad failed to offer—a home. If I need to move down here, I will.*

Trace sighs and opens the envelope he set aside. *Mom's been through enough. I need to read this first to make sure it won't hurt her.* After a brief hesitation, he braces for what he might find.

> *Katherine,*
>
> *I haven't been much of a husband and, for that matter, not much of a father. It wasn't because I didn't love you or the kids, but rather, because I don't know how to love. You were right to fear me or even to hate me. And you were right about Robbie. I didn't mean to kill him; I just wanted him to stop crying. I tossed him against the wall and thought that would shock him enough that he'd stop. Of course, he was quiet after I did that, permanently.*
>
> *I've made sure you and the kids are taken care of. That's the least I can do, and it's a way for me to say I'm sorry. You deserved someone who loved you, but instead, you got me. The few times I've known joy in my life have been with you and the kids. So, I thank you for that.*
>
> *I know I was unfair to Trace, and cruel at times. But he reminded me of your first husband. I never accepted him as mine. I realize that now. You helped him become the man he is, despite my failures, and for that, I am grateful.*
>
> *Lisa was a lovely mystery. Her fantasy world intrigued me, and I used it in my business. I knew, one day, she'd lead you and Trace to the truth. If you're reading this, then I was right.*

I wish you only the best, and I hope you and the kids will forgive me.

Yours, Eric

Trace sits back and tries to take in the words—a murder confession and a stark admission of domestic violence. He tosses the letter onto the coffee table and rushes to the bathroom. There, he grips the edge of the sink, sick to his stomach, and tries to catch his breath. Horror takes hold of his heart. *Dad truly was a monster. He killed Robbie. Oh, God.*

When Trace walks back into the living room, he paces. Back and forth, back and forth. Grim images freeze-frame in his mind. Not knowing what to do, he calls Captain Davis.

"Trace?"

"Yes, sir."

"What is it?"

"I need your advice." He weeps.

"Trace?"

"Yes, sir."

"I'm in the area. Meet me outside at my patrol car in five minutes."

"Yes, sir."

Trace grabs the evidence box filled with documentation, to leave with the captain, and carries the letter in his pocket.

When the captain arrives, he puts the box in the back seat of the cruiser and climbs into the front. The captain offers a brief smile. "You have something you want to show me?"

Trace nods.

"Let's have it."

The captain takes the letter out of the envelope and reads it. He bites his lower lip and looks out the side window for a minute before responding. "This is rough stuff."

They sit there for a couple of minutes, and the captain says, "My dad's in prison. He killed my mother. The only thing good about that man is his evil helped me decide to join the police force and put away criminals like him."

Davis pauses. "I visited him about two years ago. Seated across a table from him, I realized the man I hated no longer existed. This shell of a person I once called 'Dad' no longer held space in my heart. It was quite the revelation for me. I got out of my chair and said, 'You're a stranger to me,' and walked out.

"If I were in your shoes, I'd question whether to show this letter to my mother. Is that why you wanted to talk? Because you wonder if you should show this letter to your mom?"

"Yes, sir." Trace wipes at his soaked cheeks.

"That's your call, but if you want her to be free of any sense of guilt, failure, or regret, this letter will do it. It will affirm every fear she ever felt in her marriage, and she'll feel validated. Trace, with these words, your dad is freeing your mom to move forward with her life."

Trace glances at the captain and, red-eyed and jaw set, says, "Thank you. You're the only person I knew who'd understand."

"You call me anytime. I'm here for you, and don't forget, we meet on Friday at ten."

"Yes, sir."

When Trace returns to the suite, he seals the envelope and resolves to give the letter to his mother when he and Lisa visit later in the day.

He stretches out on the couch and thinks about his relationship with his father. Trace tries to recall one time, *any* time, when his father showed kindness to him. His imagination takes him to his earliest memories and travels through his student years. Somewhere in between, Trace falls into a restless sleep.

Ryan and Lisa wake him when they return, dripping wet. Even with beach towels wrapped snuggly around them, they leave watery footprints on the paneled floor.

"You have to go up there, Trace," Lisa says. "It's beautiful. You can see for miles—to the Sound and the mountains. Besides, the drinks are out of this world. Seriously. We had so much fun, and there were only a few guests up there."

"I can ditto that," Ryan says. "Maybe this evening we can all take a swim and watch the sunset."

"Okay, okay, you've convinced me. I'll join you for the sunset."

"Yay." Lisa cheers, thrusting her arms above her head. "We need to enjoy this place while we have it. And now, I'm going to take a shower." She looks at Ryan and arches her eyebrows, inviting his company.

Ryan beams and glances at Trace, who lifts his hands to say, *Okay by me*.

While the happy couple splashes in the shower, Trace gathers the documents and other papers related to family and stacks them by the door. He plans to put the collection in the car when they leave. The letter, he folds and pushes deep into his pocket for when he meets with his mother. Done, he walks into the kitchen and makes a vodka martini.

Situated on the deck with his drink, he flashes upon a memory of when he was five years old. His father beat him for having spilled his milk. Trace re-experiences the shame he felt along with the fear. He didn't mean to spill the drink. But from that time forward, he feared making another mistake as well as the beating that would, inevitably, follow.

Trace takes another swallow of his drink and decides he needs to visit his mother alone. He gets up, writes a note to Lisa, and leaves.

Deep in thought, Trace maneuvers the car into a free parking space at the hospital. Absorbed by a disturbing possibility, he sits still. *What would have happened if my father had survived? For sure, he would face multiple felony charges, and I would have to testify against him. The prosecuting attorney would insist on me doing so.*

Trace pictures a packed courthouse with reporters documenting the scandal. Next, his thoughts drift to his mother, bent over and weeping. Lisa sits beside her, trying to offer comfort. As Trace contemplates this scenario and the testimony he would give, he realizes his words would have destroyed any notion of family.

Did Dad choose to die to spare us this grief? Was his final act on this earth one of love?

Perturbed, he climbs out of the car, unable to silence the questions. Sudden anger assails Trace, and he kicks the front tire and shouts, "Damn you, Dad." With his head hung low, he walks through the revolving doors.

A child and his mother ride the elevator with Trace to the second floor. "I'm visiting my daddy," the child says as he fiddles with the toy superhero in his hands.

Trace smiles. "I hope he gets better soon."

"My daddy fell off a ladder, but when he's strong again, we're going fishing."

"You're a lucky young man."

Trace pauses outside the door to his mother's room and thinks about the little boy and the child's mother. Tenderness wells in his heart. *Mom did what she could to protect my innocence. There were moments*, he recalls. *Moments*. He calls out, "Hi, Mom."

Katherine sits in a wheelchair, unaided, and looks out the window. In a faint voice she says, "Trace." She reaches for his hand. He bends, kisses her, and moves a chair to sit beside her.

"I can see you're feeling better. I'm so relieved. You look beautiful. I like your new bandana. A Lisa special?"

Her happy expression communicates *yes,* and she adds, falteringly, "I'll b-be able to go h-home s-soon. Please, don't w-worry."

Trace takes her hand and fights the tears that want to flee his conflicted heart. "I have something important to show you."

Katherine studies her son. "W-whatever it i-is, we'll f-face it together."

Trace explains about the letter. His mom watches while he fingers it nervously. "R-read it o-out to me, son." It seems as though she knows its contents. When he reads the words, she grimaces and closes her eyes. At times, she tightens her hold on Trace's hand, but she doesn't cry. A single sheet of paper holds the confession for which she had prayed.

She looks at Trace but doesn't comment on the letter itself. Instead, she says, "N-now we b-begin a new l-life. One p-person's actions d-don't determine ours. There's m-much I want to s-share with you about y-your family."

"About the father I never knew?"

"Yes, and about t-the family who was always nearby. D-do you remember your c-coach?"

"Coach Rivera."

"He's your f-father's brother. We've s-stayed friends through the y-years. He'd help w-when Eric traveled."

Trace's thoughts race through the years. He remembers the coach helping him on the field and coming to the house. "Someone made repairs at home this past week. Would he have done that?"

"It's p-possible, but not j-just him. You've o-other uncles and c-cousins. R-remember Professor Teresa Jones?"

Trace nods.

"She's y-your aunt. And M-mama Maria at the Mexican r-restaurant we'd f-frequent after your games?"

"Of course."

"She's your g-grandmother."

One-by-one, Trace learns of the extended family who stayed active in his life, even though he didn't realize they were relatives.

"You are m-much loved, my d-dear son, and n-now you'll experience the breadth of that a-affection."

A knock sounds at the open door.

Trace glances up. "Coach?"

Katherine beams. "Roberto. C-come in. I just t-told Trace you're his uncle. We don't n-need to be s-secretive anymore."

Trace stands, strides to his former coach, and extends a hand, but his newly discovered uncle grabs his shoulders and offers a bear hug instead. "I'm so proud to call you *family*."

CHAPTER 22

On this early morning, Trace paces his hotel guest room, while Lisa and Ryan sleep soundly at the other side of the suite. The night before, the threesome had watched the moon rise. They'd laughed and reminisced about their early adventures together. As they did so, something shifted in Trace's heart. For the first time ever, he felt at *home*.

Trace looks over at the clock, half past five, and walks to his bedroom window. He stares into the darkness and notices hints of morning light whispering shades of orange and pink through the branches of the trees. It's too early for even the Northern Mockingbirds to sing. But it's not too early for Trace to dream.

He wonders about moving back to the area, closer to the extended family he's yet to meet. Questions about Lisa and Ryan arise—whether or not they'll remain a couple. Will they live nearby? His thoughts race, and his heart pounds. *Maybe it's time for me to follow my dreams.*

Trace gets into the shower, stands in the steamy heat, washes away his concerns, and sings—just as he did as a child.

A couple of hours later, Trace sits on the sofa in the central living area and sips his second cup of coffee. Barely awake, Ryan saunters in and rubs his eyes.

"How long have you been up, my friend?"

"Long enough for a second cup of brew."

Ryan grins. "I'll need two for sure. Last night was a lot of fun, but I had too much to drink."

"Lisa getting up?"

"I think so. At least she rolled over. Something on your mind?"

"We have a meeting with the captain, but … oh, look who's awake."

Ryan smothers Lisa with a hug and fetches cups of coffee for the two of them.

"What were you guys talking about?"

Trace says, "Not much. I mentioned you and I have a meeting with the captain this morning."

"That's at ten, right?"

"Yeah, you've plenty of time."

Lisa stretches. "I had a fantastic dream."

"One you can share?"

"Hmm, maybe not right now." She darts a mischievous smile to Ryan.

Trace clears his throat. "Well, I've thought about moving into the area." He looks at the floor and up to meet their eyes. "Last night I felt like I was home. I don't think I've ever felt that way before."

Ryan studies his friend, offers a thumbs up, and grins. "I'll help you pack."

Lisa reaches for Trace's hand. "I've considered the same thing."

A couple of hours later, Trace calls out to Lisa, "Are you ready yet?"

"I'm coming, I'm coming. What's the rush? The meeting is at ten o'clock, right? It's only a quarter after nine."

"I don't want to be late, is all. From the sound of things, this will be an important meeting."

"Let me find my sweater, and we can go."

On the way to the car, Lisa addresses Trace's impatience, "What's wrong?"

"Nothing, just a lot on my mind."

"Such as?"

"The family I didn't know I had. All the stuff I need to do to prepare the house for Mom. And if I should move back to this area. The list goes on."

"At least those concerns aren't bad things."

"True, but they still preoccupy my thoughts."

Once in the Camry, they travel in silence until Lisa blurts out, "I'm falling in love with Ryan."

Trace smirks, teasingly. "And you thought I didn't notice?"

"I thought you might, but I wanted to be sure you understood, because I've asked him to stay with me while we're at the hotel." Sheepishly, she glances at her brother.

"If you want my blessing, you have it. I'm jealous I haven't met the person of my dreams."

Trace brakes and drives into the station lot. "Let's pick up this conversation later. But from what I've seen, you two make a perfect match."

Out of the car, Lisa dashes to Trace and hugs him. "It's hard to believe, but good things are coming out of the mess Dad left. You've discovered a family. I've met Ryan. And, soon, we'll have a home again."

Lisa and Trace enter the police station and sign in, early for their meeting with the captain. In the reception area, they make themselves comfortable.

Lisa asks, "Why did he say he wanted to meet?"

"He mentioned something about documents and money."

"The cash we took from the cabin?"

"I assume so, but I don't know. He kept it vague and said he'd explain when we met."

Lisa gets up from her chair, checks out the wall plaques of city and state recognitions, and sits down again.

"Trace?" Someone calls from the hallway.

Trace looks in that direction and recognizes Becca. "Hey, Becca. This is a happy surprise."

"You're here to meet with the captain?"

"Yes, he'll be calling us in soon. I meant to call you about dinner. Still up for that?"

"Of course."

"How about tomorrow evening? Six o'clock?"

"We're on. I'll text you my address."

Trace watches her walk away, and Lisa watches Trace.

"Bro, remember my comment about good things coming from this mess? I count Becca as a positive."

Trace smiles. "I'm with you on that."

The captain approaches. "Morning, guys. Good to see you. What's it been, two days? Come on back to my office—we have plenty to talk about."

Trace and Lisa follow the captain, through multiple doors with electronic locks, to a room with an expansive desk, covered in files. The captain directs them to the leather chairs in front of the table.

"Thank you for coming. We see enough of each other that I've come to think of you as family." Captain Davis chuckles. "Besides, you still owe me a meal." He leans back in his chair, which creaks beneath his weight.

"I could have told you more over the phone. But some things are best communicated in person because they need explanation. So, let's get started.

"The local Putnam Valley Police Department, along with ours, searched your father's cabin thoroughly, inside and out. Within the cabin itself, we recovered two locked containers. One held weapons and ammunition. An arsenal. The other held an assortment of tracking devices and monitoring systems such as specialized cameras. Separately, they found more documents and papers damning to the FBI and to Schultz's trafficking operation."

He pauses and looks at them. "Your father was a complicated man. It's as if he led two lives—actually, three. All the evidence indicates an international criminal involvement."

Trace clenches his jaw, and next to him, Lisa hunches her shoulders.

Davis waves a hand in the air. "I don't have all the documentation yet, but I want to share my theory. Your father was in deep. What that was, exactly, time will tell. How he got involved, I can only guess. But there's no denying he was part of something extremely dangerous and illegal. Your dad knew his time was limited, and he made the choice to die on his terms. He defied two powerful entities and knew, absolutely, that if he didn't cooperate fully with these thugs, they'd kill him.

"So, what did he do? He planned his exit carefully. Your father played the game, but at the same time, he hid funds in an isolated cabin, and he purchased property and gold certificates. Amazingly, he protected an artifact worth millions by creating a series of complicated clues that only you two could decipher. He did all this while knowing what the consequences would be. There's the possibility he chose as he did—right over wrong—because of you."

Trace chews his bottom lip and shakes his head. "Because of us? That seems unlikely."

"If you knew you had a month—maybe less—to live, wouldn't you want to make things right?"

"I don't know. Hell, I have no clue what I feel anymore."

"Understandable. But you get what I'm saying?"

"Yes, sir."

"See that box over there? I want you to bring it to me."

Trace walks over to the box. When he struggles to pick it up, he glances at the captain.

"Try pushing it."

Slowly, Trace shoves it in front of the captain's desk.

Davis says, "This box contains over three-hundred grand in one-hundred-dollar bills. The FBI doesn't claim it, and everyone associated with Schultz is either dead or incarcerated. So, to whom does this belong? It was in your dad's safe. We have evidence of monthly payments to him from unknown sources. So, technically, it belongs to him.

"I don't know if your dad had a Will or not, but you need to check into that. And, if you end up with a windfall, you can forget the breakfast you promised me. I'll expect a steak dinner with all the trimmings." The captain holds his belly and laughs.

Lisa wipes away tears. "All this money belongs to *us*?"

The captain's features grow serious. "It was your father's. Unless his Will or Trust indicates otherwise, the money belongs to your mother."

Trace draws his head back. "I'm the Executor of my parents' Trust. It's pretty much a boilerplate document. First, the spouse inherits, and then the children."

"Hold that thought, because there's more. Do you remember the gold certificates you retrieved from the cabin?" When the siblings nod in acknowledgment, Davis says, "I performed a simple online search, and they're worth several-hundred-thousand dollars. Your names are on them, not your dad's. You need to move them into a safe deposit box ASAP."

Trace nods. "We can do that later today."

"Just a minute. I have more to explain. Your father also deeded to both of you a cottage along the Connecticut coast."

Lisa and Trace stare at him in disbelief.

"Take a look at this and read the note. There's a key taped to the paper." The captain pulls the deed from a file and hands it to Trace.

Their brows furrow while they read:

> *Trace and Lisa, your mother loves this area of Connecticut. She dreamed of having a cottage of her own. Please, take care of her when I'm gone.*

Trace covers his face with his hands and fights tears. "I've hated him for so long."

Lisa rubs his back and wipes away tears.

The captain waits a few minutes before continuing. Once they compose themselves, he tells them a story. "A while back, a preacher talked to me about redemption. He said it's like clearing debt. Action or actions a person takes to free himself from a burden. Sound familiar? I believe your father tried to redeem himself by taking actions he thought would clear his debt. I suspect that intention lies behind his final act of refusing to hand over the crown jewel. In his mind, it was payment."

Trace's lips tighten, and he thinks about what the captain has shared. "So, the jewel and money absolve him of thirty-five years of abuse?"

"No." Davis shakes his head. "But, in his mind, he saw it as payment. Absolution is another matter entirely. That's God's work, not mine or yours. I'm not a preacher type, but I've lived long enough to put pieces of a puzzle together. I conclude that forgiveness is our responsibility, and I've arrived at my own definition, which I'd like to share with you."

The captain leans forward and steeples his fingers on the desktop. "I believe forgiveness isn't about accepting bad behavior. Not about pretending a crime or injustice didn't occur. But is about untying yourself from the offender and letting him or her go."

Captain Davis studies the siblings, who sit pensively and give him their full attention. "Your father engaged in some serious stuff. You got hurt because of it. Now it's time to begin the healing process—the forgiveness that comes with letting go of the damaged person who haunts you."

Lisa takes Trace's hand and squeezes it. "Thank you, Captain, for being fatherly to us."

"Fatherly?" He laughs. "I don't know what my kids would say about that, but it sounds good to me."

Trace fidgets and taps his fingers on his knee. "Captain, what about the FBI? Last week, you inferred they'd pursue us. Will they?"

"Good question, and the answer is *no*. The Attorney General's Office has initiated an investigation. We've turned over every document and file we had in our possession related to your father's case. With that action, our work is complete. The New Rochelle Police Department has closed the case. Whatever happens, happens. We're no longer involved."

Trace crosses his legs. "And you're at peace with that?"

"I keep my heart clear. That's how I approach life. What the Feds do isn't my business and not on my shoulders. This is their case now, and I must trust they'll take the appropriate actions."

Trace nods his understanding. "Thank you, sir."

"All right. Let's move to happier topics. We have other business to take care of. Does each of you have local bank accounts?"

"Yes, sir."

"Well, let's get this box of money out of my office. You'll need to divide the funds between the two of you and deposit the cash. You'll be the custodians of this money until your mother's capable of handling it herself. In any case, it's for the three of you to work out. Of course, you must put the gold certificates into a safe deposit box. They're in your names."

Trace's eyes widen as he looks at the box of money and the stack of certificates. "I, ah, I …"

"Do you have accounts in the same bank?"

Lisa nods and rubs her brother's arm. "Yes, sir. We do."

"Simple, then. I've arranged for you to ride in a patrol car, and my officers will stand beside you until you finish the transactions. You'll make bank history today, and we don't want anything to go wrong."

CHAPTER 23

When Lisa and Trace enter the bank with police officers at their side, the branch manager springs to her feet and marches over to them. "How may I assist, officers?"

"It's these two you need to help."

The manager redirects her question, "How may I assist you?"

Trace says, "We need to make two large deposits. Also, we must place some certificates into our safe deposit boxes."

While Trace handles the details, Lisa looks around the lobby. People have stopped what they were doing and now watch the unfolding drama. A security guard walks over to the entry and remains there, alert to movements within the lobby.

The clerk takes the stacks of bills and processes them through the money counting machine. The branch manager oversees the counting—once, twice, and a final time. After completing the counting, the clerk enters the money into their accounts. Lisa and Trace accompany the manager into the vault to access their safe deposit boxes. After they've secured the certificates, they thank the manager.

"May I ask why you're making these sudden deposits?" she asks.

Lisa says, "Our father died and left us a minor fortune."

"Certainly, he's given you an amazing gift."

"An unexpected one for sure. Thank you for your help."

Lisa and Trace make their goodbyes and head back to the patrol car, where Lisa thanks the officers. "I will never forget this trip."

The officer in the driver's seat looks at his partner and smiles. "Nor will we, ma'am."

Once back at the station, Lisa and Trace thank the officers again and return to the Camry.

"What a morning." Lisa takes Trace's hand. "Why the furrowed brow? What's going on in that brilliant mind of yours?"

"There's something I need to do. Will you come with me?"

She looks at her brother's bloodshot eyes and nods. "Wherever it is, I'm with you. Here, you take the keys and lead the way."

The siblings swap places. Trace starts the car and pulls out of the parking lot. He drives east and, fifteen minutes later, pulls onto the cemetery's lane. "Where's Robbie's plot? Do you know?"

"Beside Dad's. Take the next turn." Lisa points. "You'll see it. An angel sits on the headstone."

Trace pulls over and, together, they walk to the grave, where they read the inscription on the stone:

Our beloved angel, Robbie, now plays happily in heaven.

Trace reaches into his pocket, takes out a crumpled envelope, and hands it to Lisa. "Mom and I have seen this already. It's time you read it as well."

Lisa straightens the hand-written message and studies her father's confession. Her face contorts when she focuses on one line in particular, and the next until, finally, she bends over and gasps in anguish. Trace holds her close, and they weep.

"We knew it, didn't we?" Lisa wipes her eyes and cheeks. "We knew it. But knowing it for certain … well … that's devastating."

Lisa scrubs at her chin. "I've never felt so exhausted. Every cell in my body begs for reprieve. Layers of sadness weigh down my soul, Trace, and I wonder if I'll ever laugh again."

"You will. Ryan will fill that emptiness, and with time, these memories will fade."

"It's hard to process everything. None of it seems real, but I know it is. You're right about Ryan, though. He makes me laugh."

"He's family and has been since high school. Mom loves him too."

"Aww, knowing you and Mom approve means a lot to me."

"How about we escape and venture out to the cottage we now own?"

"Yeah. I guess so. My mind's running like an express train, and I can't keep up with it. A drive will help, I'm sure."

"Maybe a beer or glass of wine over lunch?"

"I like that idea. Let's stop somewhere. I haven't eaten since early morning. You?"

"Other than coffee, nothing."

"Jamison's Hangout's on the way. We could stop there. You know the way, don't you?"

"Yeah, no problem."

They head to the Camry and Trace drives. While they navigate to the restaurant, Trace asks, "Do you accept the captain's definition of redemption?"

"I hadn't thought much about it until he brought it up. It made sense, though—payment for a debt. Words don't mean much unless they're backed with action."

"True. What about his definition of forgiveness?"

"I found it eerie. Still do. Remember what I prayed for at Dad's grave?"

"Vaguely."

"The captain almost repeated my words, and I take that as validation. When we looked at Dad's dirt mound, I prayed to let go of him, and to drop all the memories of him hurting us. Also, I told him to find a way to redeem himself and give us a reason to love him. I know it's a stretch, but strangely, I believe he might have done just that."

"Don't you think *love* is a little strong?"

Lisa exhales slowly. "If you imagine love as gushy and sweet, then yes, it's not the right word. But I imagine a *protective love* that cares enough to provide for a family."

Trace rubs the side of his head and sinks deeper into the car seat. "I don't disagree, I just need to let that notion sit with me for a while."

"Totally get that." Lisa stares out the window. "You ready to grab something to eat?"

Trace nods and navigates towards Jamison's. Once outside the car and in the parking lot, Lisa wraps her arms around her brother. "You've more to forgive than me but remember what the captain told us. *Forgiveness isn't about accepting the bad behavior.*"

At the door, Trace says, "I haven't been here since Coach Rivera joined Mom and me after a soccer game."

A server leads them to a table.

Lisa notices her brother's subdued countenance. "What's wrong?"

"Nothing. It struck me that the coach was around a lot. Sometimes, he'd take me home after the games."

"Did he do that for other kids?"

"I don't know."

"What about his children?"

"If he has any, I don't remember."

A different server takes their order, which includes a draft beer for Trace and a glass of chardonnay for Lisa.

"I asked Mom if the coach made the repairs to the house, and she smiled and said probably, but there would be others."

Lisa listens intently and leans forward. "There was a woman who would help around the house sometimes. Rosa. I remember her cleaning and singing a song over and over in Spanish, *Tres Pececitos*. She told me it was about three little fishes swimming in the sea, who needed to be careful of the big fish, which might take them away."

"I remember her well. She helped Mom after Robbie was born."

Trace glances away and back at Lisa. "Several times, she told me, 'You have eyes like your daddy.' I'd look in the mirror at my brown eyes and compare them with dad's gray-blue ones and conclude Rosa was mistaken. Now I know she didn't mean Dad."

Lisa raises her glass. "Let's toast to completing the puzzle that's been our life and starting afresh."

"Oh, what the hell. I'll toast even though I have plenty of unanswered questions."

Lisa takes a sip of wine and sets down her glass. "Let's eat, bro, and talk about ordinary things like buying new couches for the house."

"Really? You kidding? What do I know about couches? I like leather, faux or real. That's my contribution."

Lisa laughs. "Maybe you can make sure the house is accessible."

"Now you're talking."

They devour their lunch and even order a dish of ice cream for dessert.

After one more sip of wine, Lisa announces she's ready to return to Old Lyme.

"Let's do it." Trace picks up the car keys. "I'll drive. I know how you and wine tango."

"Ahh, come on. But you're right."

Trace eases into the driver's seat and steers the car onto the interstate highway. "You mentioned couches. Do you think we can furnish the house by the weekend?"

"Yeah. Shouldn't be a problem. At most, we'd have to pay extra for expedited delivery."

"Great." Trace flashes Lisa a grin. "Let's plan to have everything in place by next Friday. You and Ryan can go shopping. I'm no good at that."

Lisa laughs and shoves him. "Big brother, you don't need to convince me. Remember, I visited you at your apartment."

"All right, all right. I deserve that." The turn-off to Old Lyme comes up, and they follow the signs to the beachfront cottages.

"What's the number?" Trace peers ahead.

Lisa checks the deed. "Thirty-eight."

Trace slows so they can read the numbers on the buildings. Abruptly, he stops. "It's the blue cottage."

Trace parks in the driveway, which holds a *For Sale* sign with *SOLD* written across it. They walk up the steps and unlock the front door. It swings open to reveal a large picture window with an ocean view that takes center stage. The laminate floor paneling appears new and runs throughout the cottage. Its soft cream-and-white tones mimic that of sand.

Lisa stares, incredulous. "This is gorgeous."

They stroll through the house and comment on the special touches—the new appliances in the kitchen, the custom shower and new cabinetry in the bathroom, and the built-in shelving in each of the two bedrooms.

Trace says, "I'm going to check the garage." Lisa follows him. When he opens the door, Trace steps back. Two kayaks hang from the ceiling. Paddles and lifejackets dangle from the wall. A new washer, dryer, and sink sit at the far end, next to a built-in cabinet. And, even with all this, there remains space for one car.

Trace turns to Lisa, and his voice cracks when he says, "Dad thought of us when he purchased this place."

They step outside to the deck. From this perch, they can see Fishers Island and a long stretch of beach.

"The captain called it right, Trace." Lisa sniffs. "Dad tried to make amends in the only way he could and still protect us. Before he died, he ensured we had the resources we needed, and he gave us the cottage of Mom's dreams. Redemption? Only God can decide, but in my book, his final acts were selfless. He chose to do the right thing."

CHAPTER 24

Lisa and Trace watch with emotion as the hospital staff gathers in the hallway outside Katherine's room. Today she goes home, and they've come to wish her well. The nurses and aides hold balloons and flowers and shower her with love while an orderly pushes the wheelchair into the elevator. Katherine blows kisses in return and thanks everyone.

Radiant in a new flowered dress that Lisa bought for her, Katherine smiles and gazes up at her daughter as they approach the exit. Lisa washed and styled her mom's hair and put a dab of color on her lips.

"Thank you for everything, dear. I feel like a queen today."

Trace and Lisa accompany their mother to the waiting car and, much like walking down a nuptial aisle, they beam in anticipation of the life that awaits.

"What a beautiful day," Katherine exclaims. "I've so missed the fresh air these last weeks."

Against the backdrop of deep blue, the sun moves in and out of passing clouds. Trace points at the sky. "The forecast is for a near-perfect day, Mom, and we have some fun activities planned for you."

Trace reaches to help her get into the passenger seat, but she motions she can do it by herself, and she does. He fastens her seatbelt and closes the door.

While waving goodbye to all the well-wishers, Katherine asks, "Are you going to tell me what those planned activities are, or are they a surprise?"

Trace starts the car. "I suspect they'll be a surprise for all of us. Yesterday, a few of your friends asked if they could stop by to say hello. I told them to come."

"That sounds wonderful, dear."

"The house will look a little different to you. Lisa and I did some remodeling, and a Secret Santa gifted some specialty items."

"I can't wait to see it. Our home needed a fresh look—and a fresh start."

Lisa smiles. "Ryan and I had fun shopping for the couches and chairs. We even picked up a new dining room set. Trace selected the mattresses and worked on making sure the house is accessible. He put in grip rails and repaired the steps in and out of the house. We don't want you falling."

"I don't know what to say. You've thought of everything. I'm overwhelmed, my dears."

When they turn onto the driveway, they spot Ryan throwing a football back and forth with two teens. He gives a shout-out, and one of the young boys runs into the house to alert the others.

Katherine laughs at the sight. "I always liked Ryan. He's such a free-spirited young man. Does he have kids now?"

Trace darts a peek at Lisa, who takes the cue. She rubs the top of her mom's shoulder and says, "He's single now and doesn't have any children. He and I have been spending time together."

"Really?"

"Yeah."

Katherine chuckles and smiles at Lisa. "I'm happy for you, dear. He's good people."

A familiar woman rushes outside to help Katherine out of the car. "Rosa, I've missed you. Thank you. I'm strong enough to walk now, though I might need help with the steps."

Lisa and Trace follow close behind, ready to catch their mother should she lose her balance. As soon as the door opens, shouts of joy ring forth. Katherine looks at the gathering and wipes away tears. "My family," she says, tenderly. "I've longed to be with you more than you can imagine."

The extended Rivera family offers hugs and guides Katherine to a couch to sit down.

Lisa hears singing in the kitchen and circles in to find two women busy with lunch. One kneads dough and the other fixes vegetables. Lisa only speaks and understands a few words of Spanish, but joy needs no interpreter. She says, "Muchas Gracias."

Activity in the backyard catches her attention, and she goes to check it out.

Coach Rivera and another man stand at a grill, cooking Carne Asada. Lisa walks over to them and says, "Mm, this smells amazing. … Coach, did you make repairs to the house and landscape the yard?"

"Maybe, but even if I did, I wouldn't have done it alone." He winks at Lisa.

"Well, if you did, with or without others, thank you. Everything's beautiful."

"Anything for Katherine."

Lisa strolls around to the front of the house. Ryan waves and walks up to her.

"I told Mom we've been hanging out together."

"Hmm, don't keep me in suspense. What did she say?"

Lisa pecks him on the lips. "She said you're good people."

"I'll take that as an endorsement." Ryan bends for another kiss.

Two teenagers high-five and wolf-whistle. Trace walks out of the house at the same time and laughs. "All right, the show's over. It's time to eat!"

The boys take off, and Trace joins the love birds. "I feel like the third wheel around you two."

"Ah, poor you. Come here. Let me give you a hug." Ryan slaps Trace on the shoulder.

"Not a chance."

"What about me?" Lisa squeezes her brother. "I want a hug."

Trace nods toward the house. "Have you two noticed Mom? She's like a kid in a candy store. I haven't seen her this happy in an awfully long time."

"What about her family? Did any of them come today?" Ryan asks.

"Other than us, she doesn't have family, except a few distant cousins. She lost her parents when she was young, and she had no siblings. The Riveras were her only family until she married Dad."

"I can relate." Ryan nods toward the grill. "Shall we join the masses and grab something to eat?"

Lisa shakes her head and laughs. "You have a *thing* about food."

Ryan draws close to Lisa. "But, my dear, you trump food any day."

They stroll into the house to find controlled chaos. A couple of men sit in a corner with guitars, bellowing out songs in Spanish. Little kids dance nearby. Some adults sit, others stand, but all have a plate of Carne Asada, piled with all the extras.

"Let's get our plates." Trace leads the way to the backyard. When he sees the coach, he goes over and thanks him.

"What for? We're family. This is what families do." Coach Rivera grips Trace around the shoulders. "I'm proud to be your uncle, and now we'll see each other more often."

"I've always felt close to you," Trace says. "Long before I found out we're related. Now I have an added reason." He grins broadly and rests his hand on the coach's shoulder.

With food in hand, Trace, Lisa, and Ryan find seats at the picnic table. Lisa notices her brother's distraction. "What's on your mind?"

"The coach said we're family. I hadn't thought about it before, but it just hit me. I don't know what family means. I guess I'll soon learn."

Commotion reaches them from inside the house, and Trace stands to check it out.

Captain Davis steps out the back door. "Hey, guys. I could smell Carne Asada from the station and followed the trail." He laughs, heartily.

Trace grins and pats the captain on the back. "Wow, I didn't expect this. I'm glad you could come."

"Needed to check in on my adopted kids." The two men chat for a while, and the captain cocks his head to one side. "So, tell me, have you figured out what redemption means?"

Lisa smiles. "I think so, Captain, and you were right on target."

"What about your brother?" Davis watches Trace's reactions.

Trace stammers around and says, "I'm getting there. I've a lot to still process. But, today, I discovered my family has always been nearby. I just didn't know that to be the case."

"It sounds like the story is coming full circle." The captain studies Trace. "Have you resolved what forgiveness is and isn't?"

"Maybe. I don't think it's a one-time event for me, but if I consider forgiveness a process—" He pauses and nods, thoughtfully. "—then I'm there."

"And what does 'there' mean?"

"Harmful stuff happened. And I choose to uproot and release that from my soul. I don't want to carry it around anymore."

"I'll drink to that," the captain says. "Where's my beer?" He laughs.

Trace heads into the house, and Lisa goes with him to look for their mother. Most of the guests have dispersed, and the room has grown quiet. Katherine rests on the sofa, next to Coach Rivera. The siblings watch as the two older adults share a quiet conversation and laugh freely. When the pair lock eyes, their expressions change. A soft tenderness moves across their faces. Lisa glances at Trace. *Could it be? Is it possible they love each other?*

She contemplates the painting above the fireplace—three children with their mother. A warm feeling comes over her, and she puts her arm around her brother, who says, "We're a family again. I only wish Robbie were here with us."

Trace eases away from Lisa, grabs a drink for the captain, and moves to head back outside when a little boy runs over and wraps his arms around Trace's leg. He looks down at the kid and rubs the child's dark tousled hair.

"What's your name, partner?"

The child looks up and beams. "Robbie."

ABOUT GWEN M. PLANO

Growing up in Southern California, Gwen M. Plano loved learning, and she loved imagining stories, some grandly epic, all personal and heartfelt. She taught and served in universities across the United States and in Japan, then retired and focused again on her stories. Her first book, *Letting Go Into Perfect Love*, is an award-winning memoir recounting some of her struggles in life while providing insight into the healing process. Gwen shifted to fiction after this first book and joined forces with acclaimed author John W. Howell in writing a thriller, *The Contract: between heaven and earth*. Its sequel, *The Choice: the unexpected heroes*, soon followed -- this time a solo effort. *The Culmination, a new beginning*, is the third book of the series. Gwen lives in the Southwest with her husband, traveling and writing, sharing those stories only she can imagine. Learn more at GwenPlano.com.

Fresh Ink Group

Independent Multi-media Publisher

Fresh Ink Group / Push Pull Press
Voice of Indie / GeezWriter

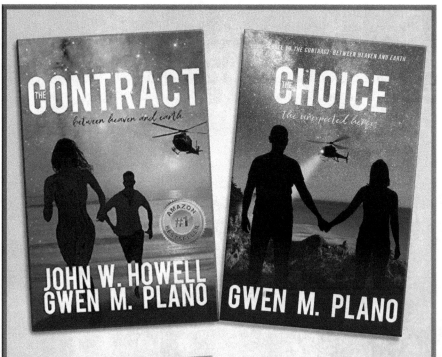

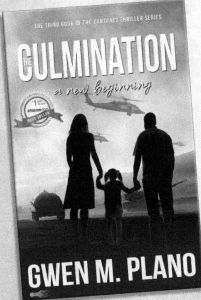

CPSIA information can be obtained
at www.ICGtesting.com
Printed in the USA
BVHW020102080223
658119BV00014B/197/J

9 781958 922170